Arissa's heart was thrumming against her chest, part from the reaction to Philippe and part from the adrenaline coursing through her body in annoyance.

She turned a corner and sighed in relief as she recognized the corridor, finding her room quickly and closing the door behind her. She took off her jacket and shoes and flung herself down on the bed. Her head was spinning.

Last time she'd kissed him he was just Philippe, the doctor who was helping at the clinic. This time she'd kissed Prince Philippe of Corinez. Did it feel different? Her heart told her no, but her brain couldn't quite decide.

And as she closed her eyes, she still wasn't quite sure.

Dear Reader,

Every girl wants to be a princess, don't they? Or do they…

For this story I got to let my imagination run riot. I got to make up not one but two countries—a fabulous Malaysian island and a European principality.

When my hero and heroine meet, sparks fly and the attraction is fast and furious, but when Philippe finally reveals he's a prince and invites my doctor heroine, Arissa, back to his principality, she has major doubts.

Arissa has fallen in love with a man, not a prince, and realizing how much comes hand in hand with his life makes her stop and consider her next steps.

But, with a wonderful family, and a hero who is willing to give up everything to love her, true love will always conquer all! Hope you love their story as much as I do.

I love hearing from readers, please feel free to contact me via my website at scarlet-wilson.com.

Best wishes,

Scarlet

ISLAND DOCTOR TO ROYAL BRIDE?

SCARLET WILSON

HARLEQUIN® MEDICAL ROMANCE™

ISBN-13: 978-1-335-64135-9

Island Doctor to Royal Bride?

First North American Publication 2019

This edition published by arrangement with Harlequin Books S.A.

For questions and comments about the quality of this book, please contact us at CustomerService@Harlequin.com.

Printed in U.S.A.

Books by Scarlet Wilson

Harlequin Medical Romance

Christmas Miracles in Maternity

A Royal Baby for Christmas

The Doctor's Baby Secret
One Kiss in Tokyo…
The Doctor and the Princess
A Family Made at Christmas
Resisting the Single Dad
Locked Down with the Army Doc

Harlequin Romance

The Cattaneos' Christmas Miracles

Cinderella's New York Christmas

Summer at Villa Rosa

The Mysterious Italian Houseguest

Maids Under the Mistletoe

Christmas in the Boss's Castle

The Italian Billionaire's New Year Bride

Visit the Author Profile page
at Harlequin.com for more titles.

For my family's own little Princess,
Taylor Hyndman. Love you loads, gorgeous girl!

Praise for
Scarlet Wilson

"There was so much to like about this book, from the charming, realistically written characters to the unflinchingly honest, medically accurate way the author addressed Sullivan's mental health issues.... I heartily recommend it as one of the best I've ever read."

—*Goodreads* on *The Doctor and the Princess*

Scarlet Wilson won the
2017 RoNA Rose Award for her book
Christmas in the Boss's Castle

CHAPTER ONE

PHILIPPE SETTLED INTO his seat and pulled his baseball cap over his eyes. It was a four-hour flight to Temur Sapora, the Malaysian island in the South China Sea, and he intended to sleep the whole way.

Two minutes later an ample gentleman tried to slide into the seat next to him. Philippe looked up briefly, shifting a little to allow the man more room to sit down. It was an instant mistake. The red-faced man instantly started talking. 'Pardon me. I'm a little bigger than the standard-sized airline seat.' He laughed, then stuck out his hand towards Philippe.

'Harry Reacher, I'm from Minneapolis in the US. Are you going to Temur Sapora too?'

Philippe let his practised face slide into place. He didn't say the word *obviously* that was floating around in his head. This aircraft had only one destination.

'Philippe,' he said simply, leaving the last

name blank. It didn't matter that this guy was American. His surname was pretty well known worldwide. The whole point of this trip was to remain anonymous—hence why he was heading to an island in the South China Sea that few people had heard of.

'I'm a doctor,' added Harry quickly, pulling a cotton handkerchief from his pocket and wiping the sweat from his brow. 'I'm going to work at one of the local medical centres for a couple of weeks. They've apparently made huge advances on wound healing.'

'They have?' Now Philippe's curiosity was definitely piqued. He sat up a little in his chair. 'What are they doing?'

There was a spark in Harry's eyes. 'You in the business?'

Philippe nodded. 'I'm a doctor too.'

'Ah-h-h.' Harry gave him a careful stare, which Philippe hoped wasn't a glimmer of recognition. 'You here to work too?'

Philippe shook his head and smiled. 'Absolutely not. This is a holiday. My first in five years. I'm going to lie low for two weeks, drink a few beers and sleep.' He left out the part about needing a bit of time and head space to regroup after his last patient in the ER. That experience would never leave him.

'If this is a holiday, where are all your

friends?' Harry looked around in surprise. 'Don't you young guys all go on holidays together?'

Philippe gave a shrug. He had years of experience at avoiding questions he really didn't want to answer. 'Thanks for the compliment but I'm not that young—thirty-one now. And I can guarantee if my friends were with me I wouldn't get a wink of sleep and that's what I need right now. Five years of fifty-hour weeks is enough for anyone. I'm starting another job in a few weeks and just wanted some downtime.'

Harry smiled again. 'And you chose Temur Sapora? It's a little off the beaten track.'

Philippe nodded. 'Which means it's perfect. Beautiful beaches, perfect ocean and an anonymous luxury resort.'

Harry shrugged. 'I guess we all need some downtime.'

'Except you. You're here to work.' He was still curious to hear about the advances in wound healing.

Harry smiled again. 'But it's for selfish reasons. I'm hoping to learn as much as I can and take it back with me. And for me, coming here, it's the trip of a lifetime.' His smile got wider. 'I can't wait.'

Philippe settled back in his seat a little as

the 'fasten seat belt' signs lit up. Harry struggled to fit his around his wide girth, eventually closing it with a bit of a squirm. 'Now,' he said. 'Where were we? Ah, yes, let me tell you about the effects of the ointment they've developed on necrotising fasciitis.'

Philippe kept a smile on his face as the plane taxied down the runway and the possibility of sleep slipped further and further from his grasp.

'Harry, are you okay?'

Three hours later Harry was rubbing at his chest again. He'd hardly touched the food when it had come and had been drinking only water. Sweat was pouring off him and his face was getting redder by the second.

'It'll pass. Just a bit of indigestion,' he said.

Philippe shook his head. 'Let me take a proper look at you.' He grabbed his backpack from under the seat in front and pulled out a tiny monitor and a stethoscope. Every doctor's first-aid kit. Before Harry could say any more, Philippe slipped the tiny probe onto his finger.

'Do you have any health conditions I should know about?'

Harry shook his head. 'Just a bit of high blood pressure but it's been under control for the last few years.'

Philippe reached over to touch him. The skin on his chest was cold and clammy. He positioned the stethoscope, knowing it was unlikely to help. Harry's lungs were functioning—it was his heart that was having problems.

'I have to be okay,' murmured Harry. 'I'm meeting Arissa Cotter at the medical centre. She's expecting me. They're down a doctor right now so the timing has worked out perfectly.' He gasped as his hand went to his chest. 'She needs me.'

For the first time Philippe could see real fear in Harry's eyes. He signalled to one of the air stewards. 'How soon until we land?'

The steward shot an anxious glance at Harry. 'Another hour.'

'Anywhere closer we can land?'

He shook his head. 'No. Not for a plane this size. There's only the South China Sea. Temur Sapora is the nearest airport from here.'

Philippe grimaced. For the first time he wished he'd taken the royal private jet. It was smaller and could probably have landed on a much shorter airstrip. But he'd wanted to be incognito—he'd wanted to have the chance of having a true holiday before he had to head back home to Corinez to take up his role in spearheading some changes in the healthcare system. The King had trained his children well.

One trained in the armed forces to be the next King, one trained as a doctor to help facilitate changes in healthcare, and one trained as an accountant to join the advisory committee on finance.

But bringing the royal jet to Temur Sapora would just have alerted most of the news agencies around the world. Not the kind of holiday he wanted.

'Give me a number for your chest pain, Harry, between one and ten.' He couldn't help it. Moving into complete doctor mode was so natural to him.

The redness started to fade from Harry's face, replaced by a horrible paleness. Harry didn't answer.

Philippe's stomach gave an uncomfortable lurch. As a doctor he'd dealt with many emergencies, but not at thirty thousand feet—and not without any real supplies. He had a horrible sinking feeling that what he needed right now was some kind of anticoagulant to stop the current damage to Harry's heart. This guy was having a heart attack. And those kind of meds weren't available at thirty thousand feet.

Within a few seconds Harry slumped over.

The steward panicked and ran to get their emergency kit and defibrillator. Philippe slid Harry to the floor. The passengers close by were wide-eyed but moved swiftly aside to let Philippe work.

Ten minutes later Philippe ran his fingers through his dark hair and let out an angry sigh. It was impossible. The defibrillator wasn't even picking up a shockable rhythm. CPR was having no effect and they were too far away from landing to continue indefinitely.

He stared down at Harry and withdrew his hands slowly, making a final check of the pulse before he glanced at his watch. 'Time of death, two-fifty-six,' he said as he shook his head. 'I'm sorry, Harry,' he said quietly. 'I guess you're not getting the trip of a lifetime any more.'

CHAPTER TWO

ARISSA GLANCED AT her watch. It was odd. Harry Reacher's plane had landed hours ago and he should have been here by now.

Her stomach squeezed. She hoped he hadn't had a last-minute change of heart. Getting doctors here was difficult enough. As it was, she used all her own holidays to cover here five weeks a year.

She finished scrubbing her hands at the sink and moved over to the small trolley she had set up. 'Okay, Adilah, let's get a proper look at that finger.'

She pulled on some gloves and touched Adilah's finger to ensure the local anaesthetic had taken effect. Her mother adjusted Adilah on her knee. 'How many stitches do you think it will need?'

Arissa gave a smile. 'I think about four will be enough. That's a nasty cut you gave yourself, Adilah. But I'll have it fixed in no time and it won't hurt a bit.'

Arissa bent down and started making the tiny stitches as she sang a nursery rhyme that her mother had taught her as a child. Adilah smiled and joined in. Within a few minutes Arissa was done, giving the wound a final check and covering it with a small dressing. She pulled out her prescription pad. 'I'm going to give you some antibiotics for Adilah, as the wound was pretty dirty when she got here. She's more liable to infection than most, so hopefully this will keep things at bay.'

Adilah's mother gave a grateful nod. Arissa noted the dark circles under her eyes. Having a five-year-old with leukaemia was taking its toll. 'Bring her back if she shows sign of a temperature or any discharge from the wound. Otherwise try and keep the dressing dry for the next few days. It should heal without any problems.'

There was a movement at the door, and Arissa looked up. Darn it. Another tourist, doubtless looking for the luxury resort that had a similar name to their clinic.

'Give me a minute.' She waved her hand as she moved to dispose of the items on the trolley and wash her hands again.

Instead of waiting at the door the curious

tourist stepped inside, nodding at Adilah and her mother as they left and then turning his head from side to side, scanning the clinic area.

Arissa felt her hackles rise. He was likely looking for luxury Egyptian cotton sheets, straw parasols, cocktails and personal waiters. This simple clinic would be something completely outwith his normal environment.

She sighed and turned around, trying her best to paste a smile on her face. 'Are you lost?' Her heart stopped somewhere in her chest. Wow. Okay, Mr Tourist was about to knock Hugh Jackman off her 'if only' list and steal his place.

Dark hair and dark eyes, combined with height and a muscular build. He was dragging some kind of backpack behind him. Not like the usual designer luggage she might have expected.

He was holding a baseball cap in his hand. He tilted his head to the side. 'Arissa Cotter?'

She blinked. This couldn't be her guy. Wasn't Dr Reacher in his sixties? She held her breath for a second. 'Who wants to know?'

Her heart started thudding against her chest as she tried to control her breathing. Was he a reporter? A private investigator? Had the secret she'd tried to hide for the last few years finally tracked her down?

The man crossed the room in three long

strides, holding his hand out towards her. 'Philippe…' He paused, then gave the briefest shake of his head. 'I'm afraid I have some bad news for you.'

She didn't like this. She didn't like this at all. She automatically stepped back and he looked a little surprised.

It didn't matter that his eyes were the darkest brown she'd ever seen. Her breath was tangling somewhere inside her, as she wondered if things were about to come crashing down around her.

She didn't answer him. Her words caught somewhere between her chest and throat.

He took a deep breath. 'I'm really sorry to tell you that I was on the plane next to Dr Harry Reacher. He had a heart attack while we were in midair.'

It took a few seconds for the words to process. 'Wh-what?'

Her brain jumped away from the fear. For a few moments she felt utterly selfish. She'd imagined this was all about her. 'Is he in the hospital?'

Something flitted across the eyes of the man calling himself Philippe and she knew instantly what came next. A horrible prickling feeling spread over her skin.

'Oh, no,' were all the words she could form.

She took a deep breath. She'd never had a chance to meet Harry Reacher but his emails over the last few months had brightened her days, his enthusiasm and passion for his work brimming over in every sentence.

The tall stranger was still standing there, watching her with those intense brown eyes. She gave herself a little shake then tried to give him a smile. 'I'm really sorry to hear about Harry. I was looking forward to working with him.' Her heart gave a little twist as she realised she'd need to carry the workload here herself for the next couple of weeks.

He nodded too and ran his hand through his thick dark hair. It was the first time she'd noticed the fatigue in his eyes. 'I'm just sorry I couldn't save him. But, up there…' he let out a sigh '…I had nothing. No drugs, proper equipment. I don't have a doubt what the autopsy will show, but I hate the fact that if we'd actually been on the ground and near a hospital, there might have been a chance to save him.'

It was the way he said the words. As if he had an edge of responsibility for what had happened.

'You had a defib?' She couldn't help but ask, she was curious.

He nodded. 'But no shockable rhythm.'

Arissa pressed her lips together. She knew

exactly what that meant. The heart attack must have been catastrophic. Whether they'd been near a hospital or not, it was unlikely that Harry would have survived.

But how many people knew it wasn't a shockable rhythm? She opened her mouth to ask when another priority sprang to mind. Of course.

She straightened up as the logical part of her brain kicked into gear. 'I should contact the hospital. See about making arrangements regarding Harry—speak to the consulate about contacting his relatives.'

'I've taken care of things,' he said, somewhat carefully.

She frowned. 'Really?'

That seemed a little odd. Regulations and red tape were notorious on Temur Sapora. Who on earth was this guy? She looked at him again. There was something vaguely familiar about him, but she couldn't place him at all. His accent was kind of strange. A mix of French, Italian and Spanish. He was definitely from Europe somewhere but she couldn't quite place the rich tone in his voice. Whoever he was, he must have money. The luxury resorts here were for the rich, the very rich and, the very, very rich.

Too expensive and exclusive for anyone less than a millionaire. At some point Temur Sapora would be found by the masses, but luckily that hadn't happened yet. She cringed every time some billionaire businessman mentioned in an interview that they'd visited a 'luxury Malaysian island' putting the spotlight on her home.

Part of her wanted the island to remain unspoiled and undiscovered. But part of her wanted it to share some of the distributed wealth of the rich visitors. The tourist resorts had given jobs to many of her friends. Families that had lived in poverty had started to gain a little income and independence. Healthcare had finally started to become a little more accessible. In the last ten years people around her had flourished. Before, Arissa had had to leave the island to train as a doctor. There was no university here, and the local hospitals weren't properly equipped. But gradual improvements had happened. She was always glad to return now and give back a little to the place she'd left behind. Her last job was in Washington, specialising in paediatrics. But the plane ride back to Temur Sapora with the familiar sight of the turquoise waters and the backdrop of the volcano always made her heart leap a little in her chest. There was no place like home.

There was a crackle above them. The guy started and Arissa gave a rueful smile. She held up one hand. 'Give it a second.'

He looked confused—his muscles tense in his neck, his hands in fists. Was he afraid? A few seconds later another noise thundered from the sky followed by a sudden torrent of rain deluging the roof above them.

A half-smile appeared on his face as he realised what the sound was, and he glanced outside at the rain thudding down on the ground. The raindrops bounced back up and the street quickly collected water. 'It almost sounded like gunfire,' he said softly.

It was a curious thing to say. Arissa glanced at her watch and shook her head. 'It's almost like clockwork.' She put her hands on her hips. 'Every day around midday we have the daily deluge.' She moved a little closer to him, catching a sea-edged scent with a hint of musk. She could feel her senses prickle. Interesting aftershave. She shifted her feet, curious and a little irritated that she'd even noticed. The rain drummed down relentlessly outside, ricocheting off the nearby roofs like a drumbeat. He'd crossed his arms across his body, revealing the muscles in his back visible through his thin cotton T-shirt.

She dragged her eyes deliberately away but immediately found them focusing on his toned, tanned arms. Darn it. What was wrong with her?

She blinked as she took a step forward so

she was slightly ahead of him. His eyes were focused firmly on the water rushing past their feet, rapidly turning a sludgy brown as it mixed with the earth from the surrounding streets.

'Is it always like this?'

She nodded. 'Yip. This is normal. Give it fifteen minutes and the sun will come back out.' She took a deep breath and pointed off to the distant volcano, currently with a dark cloud hanging over it. 'Scientists have studied it and can't really explain the phenomenon. When I was little, my *nenek* used to tell me the God of Thunder was a little sad and wanted to remind us he was still there.'

She glanced sideways at him and she could see the amused look on his face. 'And you believed that?'

Instantly she was annoyed. Her eyes went from his face to the designer emblem on the right side of the T-shirt. She recognised it. That T-shirt cost what she'd normally earn in a month. She was right. He was one of the cocky billionaires that usually frequented the local luxury resort. She'd do well to remember that instead of getting lost in a pair of deep brown eyes.

Memories flooded her brain. Someone like him would never relate to someone like her—abandoned as a baby outside a local shop. She'd been one of the lucky ones. She'd been adopted by a local couple and had a warm upbringing, only ending when they'd both died from ill health a few years ago. But she'd had to fight for everything she'd ever achieved. She loved the local stories and traditions of Temur Sapora. A man of privilege would never relate to a place like this.

She spun away and shot over her shoulder, 'Give it fifteen minutes and it'll be finished. Then, you'll be able to get to wherever you're going. If you need a taxi you'll find one at the end of the street.' She licked her lips, reluctantly adding, 'Thanks for letting me know about Harry. Have a nice holiday.'

He looked a bit stunned by her sudden dismissal. But she couldn't worry about that now. She had work to do—more, now that she knew Harry wouldn't be joining her.

She didn't have time to waste exchanging niceties with an anonymous stranger—no matter how nice he smelt.

One day. That was how long he'd been here and he was bored rigid.

The resort was glorious, immaculate and set on a gleaming white sandy beach. Every room had a view of the rippling turquoise ocean. The impeccable staff seemed to anticipate his every need. The beds and sheets were as luxurious as the ones he slept on in the palace. He had everything he could possibly want or need at his fingertips.

He'd picked the resort carefully. It was exactly what he'd wanted. A place he could completely relax and refocus. He knew after finishing his last job in a busy ER that he'd need a chance to reflect and change pace. His final patient in the ER had brought home to him just how important it was to spearhead the changes his country needed in healthcare. Corinez was a playground for the rich and famous. But not everyone who lived and worked there was rich and famous, and healthcare was something that frequently came bottom of the list on people's daily expenses. After his last case his father had promised him a few weeks' leeway before he returned to help try and develop free maternity care within Corinez.

He'd prepared for this role his whole life. He'd always known this time would come, as had his brother and sister. There was no doubt that Anthony had the hardest role—as the oldest child he was expected to take over from their father when he abdicated next year.

Philippe nodded as one of the personal concierges set a cocktail down next to him. This was his time to reflect, to plan, to take stock of what he'd learned from around the globe and apply it to the services and people in Corinez.

He had to—because paradise had changed a little over the last few years. Corinez had always been known as an island paradise. For the rich it was well known as a tax haven—the casinos flourished. Lots of celebrities had homes in Corinez. But over the last few years things had changed. The recession had hit areas of Corinez like every other country and, while the fabulously rich still existed, the people who struggled were becoming more noticeable, and those were the ones that Philippe wanted to focus on. He firmly believed that everyone was entitled to healthcare. He wanted to introduce a system in Corinez similar to the NHS in the UK. He had to start somewhere and now, more than ever, he knew that maternity care was the place to begin.

So why was he spending his time thinking about the beautiful Malaysian doctor he'd met yesterday?

Most of his dreams last night had been haunted by her dark hair, serious brown eyes, slim frame, pink shirt and dark figure-hugging trousers. He could remember every detail.

When he'd first watched her, he'd admired her easy manner as she'd interacted with the little girl. But from the second she'd realised he was there he'd almost been able to see the shutters go down over her eyes. He'd been surprised by her instantly suspicious gaze. The truth was—he wasn't used to it.

He'd spent his life in two roles. Prince Philippe or Dr Aronaz. Neither of which was usually met with suspicion. But he hadn't introduced himself to Arissa as either. Which for him was unusual. He was trying hard to keep a low profile. But now he was here?

The clientele were clearly exclusive. He'd recognised an actor hiding from a scandal. An unscrupulous politician. An author who seemed to spend all day furiously typing her latest novel. And several well-known business associates who were obviously trying to take some time to relax—even though they had phones pressed permanently to their ears.

Truth was, he really didn't want to spend time with any of these people. Particularly the blonde actress who seemed to be trying to attract his attention right now. His last experience of a relationship with an actress hadn't gone so well. She'd relished dating a prince. She'd loved the attention. The constant media coverage. What she hadn't loved was how dedicated Philippe was to his work. Or that his plans for the future had included even more work. When he'd refused to choose her over his day job she'd dumped him mercilessly. He wasn't afraid to admit he'd been hurt. He might even have loved her a little, but her hour-long interview about him on prime-time TV had killed that feeling completely. He was wary now. He wasn't ready to put his heart on the line in such an obvious way again. Here, he could just be Philippe, not a prince of Corinez. That felt surprisingly refreshing.

He looked around again. What exactly was he going to do? There was a gym—been there, done that. A business centre—no way. A beauty salon—no. A masseuse—he shuddered. He'd never been one for a stranger's hands on his skin. As for the tennis and squash courts? It was hard to play tennis or squash solo. He stretched out his arms, feeling the sun continue to heat his skin. Arissa's face flooded into his brain again.

He'd seen the disappointment on her face yesterday when she'd realised Dr Reacher wouldn't be joining her. Philippe hadn't even asked what impact that might have on her. To be honest he'd been a little stung by her sudden dismissal.

He wasn't used to being treated like that. Sure, like any doctor he'd dealt with drunk or difficult patients. As a prince he'd dealt with arrogant or obnoxious dignitaries. But Arissa?

That was something a little different. It was almost as if he'd done something to offend her—and he was sure that he hadn't.

He straightened on his sunlounger. There was a chance she could be responsible for the clinic on her own. His legs swung off the bed automatically. He took one glance at the bright orange cocktail and shook his head as he grabbed his T-shirt. He could still keep a low profile. He could introduce himself to Arissa with his Dr persona while just leaving out the part he was a prince. Temur Sapora was an island just like Corinez, albeit on the other side of the planet. Thoughts started to form quickly in his head. He could help out while learning more about their health system—treat it as a research trip. He could give her references, leaving out his last job at a hospital in Corinez. If she called there, she would find out instantly he was a prince. The others would only mention him as Philippe Aronaz.

He strode through to his suite, quickly changing as he wondered who he was trying to convince. His real focus was that slight frame and those deep brown eyes. He smiled as he strode out of the door.

No one would turn down a free doctor—would they?

CHAPTER THREE

ARISSA WAS TIRED. More than tired. The next two days were going to be the busiest. The annual carnival was due to start tomorrow and it looked as if she was going to be the only doctor available for the clinic.

It was unfortunate. She'd hoped to use technology to review some of the cases like Adilah's. There were seven kids on the island with some kind of blood cancer that she could discuss with a specialist back at her training hospital. She'd really wanted to use time to ensure they were getting the best treatments available. But now, as the only doctor at the clinic, she was unlikely to get time to do that.

She stared at the stack of photos in front of her. The clinic had negotiated sponsorship into research regarding the new ointment made from natural substances found on the island that seemed to have remarkable healing abilities. Part of her role was to help with the documentation. But it seemed that the doctor that had been here before her had fallen behind. The work was vital—the sponsorship helped keep this clinic open and full of supplies. She'd need to play catch up. It would have been possible with two doctors—particularly when Harry had been so interested in the subject matter—but now, with just her?

It didn't help that she couldn't find the digital files on the computer. If her predecessor had saved them he must have used the weirdest filing system in the world.

A shadow fell over her desk and she looked up just as her stomach rumbled loudly. Lunch. She'd forgotten about that too.

She frowned as she recognised the face. She couldn't help herself. 'Lost again? Or do you need a doctor?'

He was dressed in light trousers and a pale blue shirt. Relatively smarter than his jeans and T-shirt yesterday.

'Do you?' Was his reply.

Her brain tried to compute, but hunger and fatigue were making her grumpy. 'What?'

'A doctor? Do you need one—you know—to replace Harry for the next two weeks?'

The frown stayed in place. 'Well, of course I do. But it's not likely. So—' she pushed herself up from the chair '—what exactly do you want, Mr…?' She couldn't remember his name from yesterday.

He held out his hand towards her. 'Dr—Dr Aronaz. Here to help—if you want it.'

She stared at the outstretched hand and, slowly, put her hand out to meet his. His grip was firm, his hand warm. She ignored the little buzz up her arm. 'What kind of a doctor are you?'

'Mainly ER, but I do have some surgical experience, and I've had some obstetric experience too.'

'Where did you work?'

'I've worked lots of places.'

'I need specifics.' She couldn't help but fire questions at him. While she was desperate, she wasn't *that* desperate. She didn't want some lazy, rich guy who'd flunked out of every job that he'd had.

'I spent a spell in an ER in Chicago. I can give you my head of department's number. Before that I was in Italy in Verona, before that I was in Sarajevo in Bosnia.'

'Where did you train?'

A smile started to dance around the corners of his lips at her rapid-fire questions. 'I trained at Harvard.'

Of course. Money was practically stamped

all over this guy. She shifted her feet. But there was something else. It was old-school money.

Somehow she knew he hadn't had to work as hard as she had to get grants and loans to pursue her dream of being a doctor. In fact, she was quite sure he hadn't had to do that at all.

She was still working to pay off her loans. Goodness knew when that would finally come to an end. But it had been worth it for her. She'd achieved her dream. Her dream of being a doctor. A good doctor—a focused doctor who did the best she could for her patients. She'd even managed to introduce a system for babies who'd been abandoned like her. The safe haven project held a big piece of her heart.

People who'd trained at Harvard probably couldn't begin to understand that. She hated that money made the world go round. As a capable and competent doctor whose reputation went before her, Arissa had had more than one offer of a job if she'd agreed to work entirely privately. She'd also had a few very rich businessmen try and convince her that she wanted to work in their specialist clinics. It was almost as if they didn't understand why anyone wouldn't chase the money, and come exactly where the high salaries were.

But the biggest part of the population didn't have a high salary. As it was, she considered her normal doctor salary to be good. She didn't want to fold and end up working for the rich and famous.

She didn't need the drama. She didn't want the attention—no matter how fleeting. She was an ordinary person. And that was what she wanted to be—an ordinary person, leading an ordinary life. She'd been particularly careful not to let the media know she'd been an abandoned baby herself when she'd set up the safe haven project—she didn't want her story to be the news. This was all about the mothers and babies of now.

She folded her arms across her chest and stared up at Philippe. Mr Old-School Money. He shook his head a little. 'What's wrong? Looked like I'd lost you there. Did I say something to offend you?'

She paused, trying to find words.

Philippe filled the uncomfortable gap. He looked around. 'I'm not quite sure what services you offer in the clinic, but I'm sure my ER experience will be sufficient to give a good service. Harry told me a little of the reasons he was coming here. He was excited about a research project on healing. I'm happy to help with that too. I carried out a few research projects as part of my training.'

It almost sounded as if the guy was trying to

schmooze her. And why should he? He'd just offered his doctor services for free for the next two weeks, she should be jumping all over him. But…there was just something she couldn't put her finger on. As if there were something he wasn't quite telling her.

Arissa's instincts had always been good. She'd learned not to ignore them.

'What kind of projects?' She didn't quite mean the way the words came out—as if she didn't quite believe him.

But he kept his cool even though he looked slightly amused by her questioning. 'I did one in West Africa looking at polio and smallpox vaccination, encouraging uptake. It was hugely successful. I did another in London, working at a specialist centre that diagnosed PoTS—you know, postural orthostatic tachycardia syndrome. Fascinating.'

She pressed her lips together. He'd gone from one end of the spectrum to the other. If the guy actually showed her his résumé she was pretty sure it was far more impressive than hers.

A pager started sounding at her waistband.

Oh, no.

He wrinkled his nose. 'What is it?'

She started moving, crossing her room and grabbing her jacket and keys. 'We need to go. We need to go now.' This was exactly the reason she could do with another doctor. She tried not to smile as she turned her head. 'If you want to start—Dr Aronaz—you start now.'

Philippe was slightly confused. He watched as Arissa changed her flat shoes for a pair of runners and pressed the button on her pager to stop it sounding. A pager in a community clinic? He wasn't quite sure what that meant. Community clinics didn't normally cover any kind of emergency service.

Arissa didn't hang around. She was out of the door in a flash. For the briefest of seconds he'd felt as if he'd had to convince her to let him work alongside her. He still wasn't entirely sure she *had* agreed to it. What was it about him that put her hackles up?

For another few seconds there he'd thought she was almost smiling at him. But, it had vanished in an instant. And she was already climbing into the old-style Jeep that sat outside the clinic. He didn't hesitate. He climbed in next to her.

'Where are we going?'

She didn't answer as she started the car and pulled out onto the road, glancing at her watch.

He looked around him. 'Do we have any supplies?' If they were heading to some kind of accident they'd want a minimum amount of supplies.

She pressed her lips together. 'There's an emergency kit in the back. Hopefully we won't need it.'

He leaned back into the seat, still trying to work out what was going on. The streets of Temur Sapora blurred past. Arissa kept glancing at her watch, going around a few corners practically on two wheels. Philippe gripped the handle on the inside of the door. Wherever it was they were going, she wanted to get there quickly.

He frowned as they pulled up outside a fire and rescue centre. The front door was down, the rescue truck visible through the upper windows. It didn't look as if it was going anywhere. Whatever they were doing it didn't involve other emergency services.

Arissa jumped out of the car and ran over to the wall. A few seconds later another black car pulled up alongside them. A fire and rescue guy jumped out too; he nodded at her. 'Arissa.' His footsteps slowed. 'Let's see what we've got.'

Philippe was more confused by the second. 'What on earth are we doing here?'

Arissa looked over her shoulder towards him. 'Lim, this is Dr Aronaz. My temporary workmate for the next two weeks.' She pulled a key from her pocket. 'Okay?'

Lim gave a nod and stood alongside Philippe, staring at the red panel on the brick wall expectantly.

There was a noise. Something he didn't expect. His stomach clenched. Was that a baby crying? Lim glanced at him, realising his confusion.

He pointed to the pager on his belt, then gestured towards the red panel that Arissa unlocked and pulled towards her.

'This is our safe haven. A place that someone can come and leave their baby. No questions asked. As soon as a baby is left, our pagers go off. We aim to get here within five minutes.'

Philippe couldn't move. He was fascinated. Arissa slowly pulled out the red panel in the wall, and he realised it was a carefully constructed shelf. Inside was a squirming baby, wrapped in a thin cotton blanket. Arissa lifted the baby out gently. 'Hello, honey,' she said quietly, gathering the baby in her arms, and stroking its head with one light finger. The baby instinctively turned its head towards her finger—rooting. Trying to find food. This baby was hungry.

Philippe stepped forward, his curiosity too much for him. Arissa nodded. 'Get me a pack,' she said to Lim, who disappeared and grabbed something from the boot of the Jeep.

Arissa carried the baby over to the Jeep and laid it down gently in the back, opening the blanket and giving the baby a quick visual check. The umbilical cord was tied with a piece of string and the baby was still smeared in some vernix. 'It's practically a newborn,' Philippe said, looking over her shoulder.

'Do you have much experience with newborns?' she asked.

He gave a little shrug. 'I've delivered three babies in the ER.'

She zipped open a tiny pack, pulling out a tympanic thermometer, a collection of wipes, and a tiny finger probe. 'Give me a hand,' she said quickly.

The baby started to squirm. Lim stood back and let Philippe move forward. He pulled a pen torch from his back pocket—it was amazing the things you kept on you when you were a doctor—and leaned forward, doing a quick check of the baby's pupils. They had no idea how this baby had been delivered, or if there had been any trauma. 'Both pupils equal and reactive,' he said, doing a manual APGAR score in his head. The skin colour was good, muscles reactive, the baby kicking as he examined it. He slipped on the finger probe and glanced at the screen for a reading. 'Do you have a stethoscope?' he asked Arissa. She smiled and pulled a bright pink stethoscope from her pocket.

'Don't you believe the monitor?' she asked.

He smiled as he took the stethoscope. 'I like to do things the old-fashioned way,' he said. The monitor reading said a pulse of one-forty and an oxygen saturation of ninety-eight per cent. This baby was doing fine.

He listened for a few seconds, checking the lungs, making sure the baby hadn't inhaled anything untoward during delivery, then listening to the heart, checking for any heart murmurs or any other abnormality. He hoped Arissa couldn't see the beads of sweat breaking out on his forehead. An abandoned baby, albeit in a safe place. This was bringing back so many memories for him—of a baby that wasn't healthy and pink like this one.

The baby let out an angry yelp as he lifted the stethoscope away from its chest. He did one final check. 'Well, she seems like a perfectly healthy little girl.' He inadvertently tucked the stethoscope into his back pocket. 'I just hope mum is doing so well.' His stomach squirmed as he said those words.

Arissa turned her eyes to Lim, who gave them both a nod. 'I'll put the word out. You okay?' he asked.

Arissa nodded as she wrapped the baby back up and put her to her shoulder. 'I think we'll be good. I'll take her back to the hospital and get her admitted and fed.'

Lim unlocked the door to the fire and rescue station and came back out a few minutes later with a car seat in his hand. He nodded towards them both. 'I'll leave you to it. Will let you know if we hear anything.'

He climbed into his black car and disappeared into the distance. Philippe turned to Arissa, his mind whirling. He pointed to the red panel on the fire station. 'What on earth is this?'

Arissa tossed her car keys towards him. 'It's a safe haven. We set it up last year. Someplace safe that a woman can leave her baby. No questions. No prosecutions. An alarm goes off as soon as the panel is opened.' She shook her head as he frowned and looked above the panel. 'Not at the station,' she said and pointed to her belt. 'To our pagers. There's always a doctor and a member of the fire and rescue crew who have the pagers. One, or both of us, aim to get here within five minutes.'

Philippe was still surprised. 'How many babies does this happen to?' Why hadn't he heard of this before? This was exactly the kind of thing he needed to know about. Ideas were already forming in his head.

Arissa gave a shrug. 'There's only been three since we started. But having a safe haven to leave a baby is organised in lots of places.' For a second he thought something flickered across her face but she pressed her lips together, then started talking again. 'When I was a little girl, there was a baby left outside the old clinic. It was there all night. The clinic isn't staffed overnight and I'm not sure that people knew that. Anyway, the baby nearly died. My mother told me about it. Everyone was upset. They never found out whose child it was. But the story stayed with me. And over the years I've often thought it should be something that we should start here.' There was something in the way she said the words that sounded a little off. From the little he knew of her, Arissa normally seemed quite comfortable, but those words had come out hard and stiff.

But Philippe was frozen to the spot as the memories flooded through him again. So many things about this were familiar. Only a few weeks ago something similar had happened in Corinez. But Corinez had a different climate from Temur Sapora. The baby left in Corinez had suffered from hypothermia. It had been touch and go. Philippe had been on duty. He'd spent the next two days trying to revive the child and had failed. He'd never lost a child before and it had moved him in ways he'd never expected. It had seemed such a random act. And it had enforced for him even more the glaring need for free maternal healthcare in Corinez. Had the mother not presented at hospital because she couldn't afford to pay the bill? Maybe she had no help at home. Maybe she hadn't known she was pregnant, or hadn't told anyone. Whatever the reasons were, try as he might, he hadn't been able to track her down to ensure her safety. He'd asked questions around the hospital. It hadn't been the first abandoned baby—but it had been the first who'd been exposed to adverse weather conditions. Maybe it was time to set up a scheme like they had in Temur Sapora?

'They have these all over the world. In France, the USA, Italy, Hungary, Russia, Japan, Switzerland and the Philippines. They have a whole host of names—baby windows, baby cots, cradles of life, safe havens. But they all have the same function. A safe place for a mother to leave a baby.'

She fitted the car seat into the back of her own car and climbed in next to the baby. Philippe looked at the car keys in his hand and gave a little shake of his head as he climbed into the driver's seat.

'The fire station here isn't always staffed and it's in a quieter street. That's why we decided this was a more appropriate place than the clinic. If someone wants to leave their baby, they won't do it while the world is watching. Our clinic is right in the middle of the main street. The rest of the crew who work here are on call. So, someone will always be able to attend quickly to any baby left in the safe haven.'

He started the engine. 'I take it I'm driving you both to the local hospital?' His brain couldn't stop turning over and over.

Arissa was bending over the baby strapped into the back seat. She looked up and smiled. 'Well, look at that, little Dee, our new doctor is a resident genius.'

He sighed and smiled as he shook his head. 'Dee?'

She nodded as he followed the signs on the road to the local hospital. It was only a few minutes away. 'This is our fourth baby. The first two were boys. We decided just to go with the alphabet. Our first was called Amir, our second Bahari. Our third baby was a girl. We called her Chi-tze, and this time, we'll pick a name beginning with D.'

Now he understood. 'The babies never have

a letter or a note? Something to tell you what their name is.'

He was doing his best to keep his eyes on the road. But he couldn't help but glance over his shoulder at the woman with dark curls looking down at the tiny baby. He could see the compassion and empathy in her face, making his stomach twist in a way he just hadn't expected.

She gave a sad kind of smile as she stroked the little girl's face. 'Not yet,' she sighed. 'I wish they would.'

'Have you ever managed to reunite a mother and baby after they left the baby at the safe haven?'

Arissa shook her head. 'I'd love to tell you yes, but the honest answer is no. For two of the babies we never found their mother. Another one, she got admitted with an infection. But...' he could hear the waver in Arissa's voice '... she didn't want to be reunited with her baby. She had a difficult history. Even with the offer of support, she just didn't want to go down that road.'

Philippe turned into the hospital and found a space in the car park. He switched off the engine and turned around. Arissa was talking quietly to the baby. 'So, have you picked a name yet?' he asked quietly.

She glanced over at him. There was a smattering of freckles on her pale brown skin, over her nose. Her eyes were the deepest brown he'd ever seen. It was almost as if they sucked him in, holding him in place. For the briefest of seconds their gazes locked in a way that made him hold his breath.

'I think you should pick the name,' she replied, the edges of her lips turning upwards. 'As long as you stick to the rules and pick something with a D.'

He got out of the car and walked around to her side, opening the door and looking down at the little baby. Her face wrinkled and she let out a yelp. He reached down and picked her up as Arissa released the harness on the car seat. He put the baby on his shoulder and patted her back as she continued to yelp. 'I think she's hungry,' he said with a smile. Then something else crossed his mind. 'We don't even know if she's been fed at all. Maybe we should hurry up with the admission process and prioritise the food.'

Arissa closed the car door and walked alongside him. 'I think we can manage that.' She gave him a wink. 'I might know someone.'

It was the oddest feeling. This morning he'd been lying at a luxury resort with two weeks of fine dining and relaxation ahead of him. Now, he had a tiny newborn baby snuggling into his neck and—from what he could feel—currently trying to latch on to him. A beautiful woman, surrounded by the scent of freesias, was walking next to him and making him strangely curious about her, and this place.

It was the oddest sensation. He'd thought he'd wanted to come here to sort out how he felt about the next part of his career—the next part of his life. But here he was, volunteering to work on a day job. Wanting to spend the next two weeks finding out more about this woman and this place.

He almost laughed out loud. No wonder his ex had complained he couldn't switch off from work. He just didn't want to. Being a doctor and doing his best for other people was ingrained in him, running through his veins in his blood.

As they walked inside the front doors of the hospital he turned to Arissa. 'Hey, I don't know any Malaysian names. I can't pick a name for this little cutie.'

'Give it some thought. You're about to meet a million new people.' She wagged her finger at him. 'I'll warn you now, they'll all start campaigning for their own name.'

His footsteps faltered a bit. He wasn't quite sure what she meant. 'They'll know we're looking for a name?'

He looked down at the little face. So innocent. So pure. A little girl abandoned by her mother for a million reasons he didn't know about.

Arissa reached over and touched his arm. He almost jerked at the feel of her warm fingers on his skin. 'Our babies are special,' she said softly. 'Everyone in the hospital supports the safe haven project. As soon as they see us, you'll feel like a superstar.'

There was an edge to the way she said the words. A touch of sadness. He looked at her curiously. 'Does the publicity help?'

She shuddered. She actually *shuddered*. 'No. We don't talk outside the hospital about the babies. We don't want to do anything to compromise the safety of the person who has left their baby. It's just internal. Word spreads fast. Everyone always comes to see the new baby.' She sighed. 'There's a lot of love around here. By tomorrow, they'll have an emergency foster carer ready to take her.'

He gave a nod. Did they have all this set up in Corinez? Was this something he could add into his newly purposed health system? His brain was spinning. He had to make some links. He had to talk to some of his advisors—and to some of the staff and ministers he would be working with.

It was weird. He'd resigned himself to this

new life. But he'd never really felt the spark of excitement for it that he did now. The truth was he'd felt a little bitter about his future plans. Or maybe bitter was the wrong word, maybe it was overwhelmed. It was easy to work as a doctor somewhere and complain about lack of supplies or long hours. To be tasked with trying to implement change in a system that was so focused on finance? That was something else entirely. Free healthcare—even just maternity systems—would cost Corinez in a way that hadn't been experienced before. He had to pitch things just right.

The one thing he was sure about was that he wanted to do well.

And for the first time, things were starting to take shape in his mind.

Thanks to this. Thanks to Harry. Thanks to Arissa.

Her hand was still on his arm and it tightened a little as they walked through the next set of doors. She gave him a smile. Ahead of them was a whole heap of expectant waiting faces. Nurses, admin staff, kitchen aides and cleaning staff were all standing at the nursing station.

'Word does travel fast, doesn't it?' he said in wonder as they all started walking towards him.

'Welcome to Temur Sapora,' Arissa said as she raised her eyebrows.

* * *

Philippe surprised her. Of course, she'd pulled out her phone and emailed and checked his registration and references—which were all glowing. There was a small gap in the dates in his CV. But she wasn't concerned. Lots of doctors took a few months out at some point in their lives. Maybe that was why he was here?

After he'd done the obligatory baby checks under her scrutinising gaze, she'd almost expected him to disappear back to his luxury resort. But no.

He stayed at the hospital while the paediatrician did their own assessment of the little girl then admitted her overnight for observation. Instead of leaving, Philippe settled down in a chair next to the cot in the nursery. He even asked if he could give the baby her first feed, which she gulped hungrily.

He wasn't flustered when crowded by all the other staff who were anxious to see the new baby. In fact, he dealt with it like an old pro, smiling, answering politely and giving everyone a chance to see the new arrival. But what she did notice was the way he expertly circumvented answering specific questions about himself. It made her curious because she recognised the skill—it was something she'd done herself on occasion. How much did she actually know about this guy—apart from the fact he was a real doctor with good references? She made a note to try and find out if he'd been working in the last few months—that was where the gap in his CV was.

Eventually, they were left alone to get the baby settled. She still had half a mind that Philippe would make an excuse and go back to his bed in the luxury resort. But he didn't. He finished feeding the baby and changed her nappy, all the while firing questions at Arissa about the safe haven scheme and the outcomes for babies like this.

They finally settled on a name—suggested by one of the nursing staff—Dian.

Philippe rested back in the wide armchair and nestled Dian into the crook of his arm, stroking his finger across her forehead and down her nose. 'Well, little Dian, you've had an unusual start in this life. But you're here, you're safe, and hopefully your mum is too.'

Arissa could see a million things swirling around in his mind. Part of her wondered if a man who obviously came from money would be judgemental about what led a woman or girl to abandon their baby. But nothing like that came from his lips. All she could read on his face was empathy and part of her heart swelled in her chest at his reactions to little Dian.

In fact, he'd really surprised her. He sat there all night, asking a few questions about what would happen now with Dian, but mainly just holding the baby and talking to her.

'Aren't you tired?' Arissa asked finally.

'Sure.' He shrugged, but his dark brown eyes still had a bit of sparkle in them. 'But no more than usual.' He looked around. 'And this...' he smiled down at Dian '...is different. How many times as a doctor have you cursed yourself because you haven't had enough time to do something? How many times have you wanted a few more hours just to spend with a family, and give them some comfort?' He gave a little nod as he looked at Dian again. 'Tomorrow, Dian will go to a foster family, who'll hopefully have all the time in the world to support her. But for now...' his gaze met hers again '...it's you, and me.' Dian gave a little whimper and he tucked her up onto his shoulder and gently rubbed her back. 'And let's face it—this isn't so bad?' He stretched out his legs and put them on the low table in front of him. 'What else would a guy do? Eat fancy dinners? Drink champagne cocktails?' He winked. 'That is how you think I spend my time, isn't it?'

Her stomach gave a little flip. Maybe it was time to start making her facial expressions less obvious. 'I didn't say that.'

'Yeah.' He nodded, a gleam in his eye. 'You did. But let's just call it getting-to-know-you time.'

Heat rushed into her cheeks and she gave an embarrassed shudder, before biting her bottom lip and trying to get comfortable in the chair next to him.

She didn't want to leave Dian either. It just seemed wrong that this poor little girl would spend her first day on this earth without someone to cuddle her during the night. The hospital staff knew her. They weren't the least surprised to see her settle in for the night, and a few were already casting interested glances in Philippe's direction. By morning, tongues would be wagging. She'd just have to make sure she introduced him formally as the temporary clinic doctor.

He was singing. And it totally wasn't what she'd expected.

But to be honest she wasn't sure what she'd expected at all. All the preconceived ideas she might have had about her upper-class guest were rapidly disappearing out of the window.

They'd come straight here from the hospital and had a quick chat first thing about the types of patients who normally attended the clinic. Temur Sapora had once had a mining industry, so chest complaints were common in the older population. Philippe had volunteered to see all the respiratory complaints and he seemed to be doing well. Until she heard him singing...

She pulled back one of the curtains. 'What is that?' She couldn't help but ask.

Philippe was sitting next to an elderly local man whose shirt was open. Philippe had a stethoscope pressed to the man's chest and both were singing along and laughing. Philippe turned towards her. 'That,' he said in mock horror, 'is Frank Sinatra. You mean you didn't recognise it?' He tutted and shook his head. 'Youngsters these days, Rahim. They don't recognise one of the greats when they hear it.'

Arissa couldn't help the smile on her face. 'Oh, I recognise the greats, but no one could recognise that,' she said.

Rahim erupted in laughter, than started coughing and spluttering. Philippe shot her a look and stood up, moving to the nearby sink to wash his hands. 'It looks like Rahim has another chest infection. We were trying singing to see if it could help his lung capacity.'

He was choosing his words carefully. It was clear that Rahim, like many of the people around here, had chronic obstructive airways disease. His colour was poor and his breathing rapid. Any delay in treatment could end up in a hospital admission. Philippe moved over to the medicine cabinet. 'I'm going to dispense some antibiotics for Rahim to take away with him, so we can get him started on treatment without delay.'

She liked the way he was obviously trying to put the man at ease.

Now she really did smile. He knew that for a patient like Rahim, writing a prescription that would have to be taken to a pharmacy and dispensed wasn't the way to go. More often than not, patients like Rahim wouldn't fill their prescriptions. Some might assume it could be down to cost—and it could be, but not always. Other times some of the older patients didn't want to be a nuisance, or forgot to fill their prescriptions. There was a whole variety of reasons. But Philippe was doing exactly what she would have done—making sure the medicine was in the hands of the patient who required it.

The very fact that she didn't have to explain any of this to Philippe made her wonder about him a little bit more.

She gave him a nod and let him finish, moving on to the next patient.

A few hours later he appeared behind her, an empty coffee cup in his hand. 'Okay, I've snagged a cup. But where do we find the coffee?'

She glanced out at the waiting room that had

finally quietened after her morning's immunisation clinic.

She gestured with her head. 'Come on. I'll take you to the magic.'

She led him through to the small kitchen at the back of the clinic, switched on the percolator and flicked open the nearest cupboard, which was stocked from top to bottom with a variety of coffee.

Philippe blinked, then laughed. He lifted his hand. 'What is it? Did some kind of rep come here and give you his whole supply?'

Arissa folded her arms and leaned against the wall, watching him for a few moments. 'Maybe. Or maybe it's just a rule that every doctor that works here has to buy their favourite kind of coffee before they leave.'

His eyes widened. 'Exactly how many doctors have you had working here?'

She gave a sigh. 'A lot. There are no permanent doctors here. Haven't been for years.'

He frowned as he pulled one of the packets of coffee from the cupboard, gave it a quick appreciative sniff and loaded it into the machine. 'So how on earth do you keep things running?'

She shook her head as she grabbed another mug. '*I* don't. We...' she held out her hands '...the community does. I commit all my holidays to working here.'

He stared at her for a few seconds. 'All of your holidays?'

She nodded. 'Sure. Have done for the last five years. Temur Sapora is home. This is where I'd come for my holidays anyway—so why not come here and work? We have lots of volunteers. Though I have to admit that the wound-healing project has definitely been a boost.'

The smell of coffee started to fill the room. 'So, you're telling me that this whole clinic is staffed by volunteers?'

She smiled. 'Yes, and no. There are three permanent nursing staff and two administrators. They're actually the most important people of all—they handle the rota.'

'So, there are more doctors like you?'

She could see just how many questions he wanted to ask.

She nodded. 'There's no university training for medicine on Temur Sapora. Anyone who wants to train as a doctor has to leave.'

He tilted his head to the side. 'And no one wants to come back full time?'

She instantly felt her hackles rise. He probably didn't mean to offend but she couldn't help how she felt.

'Hey.' He moved in front of her, his fingertips connecting with her arm. As she breathed she inhaled his sea-edged aftershave. 'That didn't quite come out the way it should.'

For a few seconds she didn't move, conscious of the expanse of his chest moving up and down under the pale blue shirt right in front of her face. She hadn't realised she was quite so short compared to him. She tipped her head upwards. Now she was this close, she could see the emerging stubble on his jawline—apparent after a night spent in the hospital. It rankled that he still managed to look this good with no real sleep or a change of clothes. It suddenly made her conscious of her own appearance.

His dark brown eyes smiled down at her apologetically. 'Sometimes things just come out a little awkwardly,' he said.

'They didn't seem to earlier. You had all the hospital staff practically sitting in the palm of your hand. Charm seemed like your main offensive.'

'Ouch.' He laughed, then ran his fingers through his dark hair. He hadn't moved. He was still only a few inches from her. 'I guess when I'm tired then the charm slips.' He held out both hands. 'What I meant to say is that I'm impressed. I've only been here two days and I'm impressed already. By the clinic, by the safe haven project. You're making me think about things. Work I could do back home.'

She wrinkled her nose. 'Aren't you supposed to be on holiday?'

'What can I say? I got bored.' The percolator started to bubble and this time he did step back.

It was the oddest sensation. She was almost sorry that he did.

She blinked and turned away, feeling instantly self-conscious. She fumbled in her trouser pocket to find a ponytail band, then tried to capture the errant curls that had escaped around her face. She pulled her hair upwards, then stared down at her wrinkled pink shirt. 'Maybe I should take five minutes and go home and change.'

He handed her a cup of steaming coffee. 'Why? You look fine. Gorgeous as ever.'

Her stomach clenched. The man who'd displaced Hugh Jackman from her 'if only' list had just called her gorgeous. As soon as the thought appeared in her head she pushed it away. She didn't have time to think like that. There was too much work to be done. Too many other things to sort out. He might be a doctor, but he was still a tourist. Temur Sapora would be just a fleeting visit to him. Nothing more. Nothing less.

She pulled herself back to the conversation from earlier. 'If I came back here permanently, then I'd have to work as a generalist. I've spent the last year specialising in Paediatric Oncology. It's where my heart lies. But because there's a smaller population on Temur Sapora there wouldn't be that opportunity to specialise.' The aroma of coffee was drifting around her, overpowering the teasing smell of his aftershave and allowing her to concentrate again. 'It's the same for the rest of my colleagues who volunteer here. One is a surgeon, another a cardiologist, another an endocrinologist. In fact—' she gave a little smile '—we probably cover just about every speciality that there is—and that has its benefits too.'

She glanced through the glass-panelled door to the waiting room outside. It was the first time in days there hadn't been a number of patients waiting to be seen—partly because Philippe was proving so useful. She gave a little nod and sat down on the comfortable sofa in the staff room. 'There's a few children whose cases I can review and treatment plans I can look over while I'm here.'

Philippe settled onto the sofa beside her, his thigh brushing against hers. 'They don't go to the mainland for treatment?'

She shook her head. 'The mainland is a four-hour flight away. The truth is it's expensive, and it's not just the flights. It's the hospital treatment once you get there, and room and board for the families. It all adds up.'

He took a sip of the coffee, sighed and rested back on the sofa, closing his eyes for a second. 'You're right, it does. I guess none of us has really mastered the healthcare system yet of our countries.'

It seemed an odd thing to say. She let out a little laugh. 'And why would that be our job? We just have to work in the system. Not design it.'

It was as if she'd just given him a sharp jab. His eyes flew open and he sat bolt upright again. 'What? Oh, of course, yeah. You're right.'

She frowned. 'Dr Aronaz? Are you okay? Do you want to get some sleep?'

He shook his head. For the briefest of seconds he'd had that rabbit-caught-in-the-headlights kind of look. But he seemed to shake it off as quickly as it had appeared. This guy had a real talent for smoothing things over.

Something prickled in the back of her brain. Something vaguely familiar that she just couldn't place. But before she could think about it any more, Philippe had turned to face her. 'Hey, we haven't had a chance to discuss the research project on wound healing yet. Why don't you run me through it and tell me what you need me to do to assist?'

Of course. For the last few days there hadn't really been a chance to keep things as up to date as she wanted. The project was proving really successful and it was vital she made sure the research was recorded accurately. If things worked out, it could eventually lead to better funding for the clinic. She had to keep the long-term goal in mind. She set down her coffee and pulled over a laptop from the nearby counter. 'Sure, let me show you what we're doing…'

CHAPTER FOUR

HE WAS TIRED. He was more than tired. But being around Arissa was keeping him on his toes. She seemed to be the adrenaline shot that he needed to keep going.

She'd checked his references—of course she had. But he'd been lucky that a quick call to the palace had resulted in them arranging an emergency visa for him to work in Malaysia—so all his credentials had been in order.

The research here was fascinating. The locally made, natural ointment was producing worthy results. He predicted as soon as this research was published there would be a variety of manufacturers vying for their attention.

Leg ulcers were a worldwide problem. Generally a product of old age, a deteriorating circulatory system and lack of mobility, they were one of the most chronic, slow-healing wounds to deal with. Philippe had encountered patients before who'd had leg ulcers for years that sometimes showed a few signs of healing, then broke down all over again. So far the ointment they were using on Temur Sapora was showing remarkable results.

The data collection was meticulous. He'd reviewed six of the patients using the ointment today, and another six patients who were being treated with an alternative ointment. Photographing the wounds, documenting the treatment plans and recording the patients' observations had actually been kind of fun. It had been years since he'd been involved in any kind of research study, and this one had real promise.

He stretched his arms above his head as Arissa came into the room. 'Are you done?'

She put a hand on his shoulder. He nodded. 'Just finished. It's taken me back to my student days, and I forgot how much I love all this stuff.'

She gave a tired smile. 'I just wanted to say thanks. You doing this has given me a chance to review the kids I wanted to.'

He could see the tiny lines around her eyes. 'All good?'

She pressed her lips together. 'One is sicker than I hoped and doesn't seem to have responded well to treatment. I've made some recommendations for changes.'

'Would the kid have done better on the mainland?'

He could see her muscles tense. 'Maybe. Who knows? But the rest of the family wouldn't. There's only Mum. And she has four children. If she'd taken her son to the mainland, she would likely have had to leave the others behind.'

He gave a slow nod. He knew exactly what she didn't want to say. Although many child blood disorders were now curable—not everyone had the same outcome. He could tell this case was bothering her.

He stood up. 'Come on,' he said.

She looked confused. 'What?'

He leaned over and grabbed his jacket, shutting down the computer quickly. 'It's been a long day. I'm going to shout you dinner.'

She shook her head. 'You don't have to do that.'

'Yes, I do. Come on.'

She shook her head again. 'No. It's late, you must be tired. You've already given up your holiday.'

He extended his hand out towards her. 'As have you.'

He wasn't going to listen to any of those half-hearted excuses. He'd only had a glimpse of the type of person that she was—and it was enough. She'd had to move away to study. Her long-term career path couldn't be here—but that didn't mean she wasn't prepared to give up all her holidays in order to pay back a little to the place she called home.

If he was tired—how was she?

When was the last time Arissa Cotter had been pampered? Taken out for dinner? Looked after?

There was something behind those eyes that he hadn't got to the bottom of. And after only a couple of days he couldn't expect to. But that didn't mean that he wasn't curious.

She hadn't taken his hand yet. 'Do you really want to go back home and eat barbecue snack noodles?' he teased.

She sighed, then laughed. 'Actually I planned to have frozen pizza and some candy bars.'

He put one hand on his hip, leaving his other hand deliberately still extended. 'Oh, it was one of those kind of nights.'

She shrugged. 'Maybe. I hadn't quite decided yet.'

'Well, I have. I spotted a restaurant in the next street over I want to try.'

Her tired eyes twinkled. 'Which one?'

He looked directly at his outstretched hand. 'You have to agree to come before I tell you.'

It was almost like a stand-off. She reached

for her denim jacket and put her hand in his. 'How about you let me pick your dinner?'

Right now, he'd agree to any terms. 'What, you know the boss? You get a discount?' he joked.

She rolled her eyes. 'Like you need one.'

His stomach gave a tiny twist. Maybe he wasn't as incognito as he'd thought.

Fifteen minutes later she'd ordered all her favourites. Homemade *roti canai*, *roti telor* and curry chicken, Indonesian fried rice and seafood soup. The aroma made her stomach rumble loudly and he turned towards her and laughed.

She gestured towards the array of dishes on the table. 'You asked for recommendations.'

His eyebrows rose. '*All* of them?'

'Absolutely. Dig in. The food here is the best around.'

Philippe didn't hang around, he filled up his plate and sampled everything.

She couldn't help but watch him. He'd changed just before they came here and the black polo shirt made his eyes seem even darker. He signalled to the waiter for some wine and waited until they both had a glass.

She took a sip and leaned back in her chair.

'When was the last time you actually relaxed?'

'What do you mean?'

'I can practically see the knots in your shoulders.'

She shook her head. 'No, you can't. And I told you, this is what I like to do on my holidays.'

'But then you're never really not working.'

She took in a deep breath. 'I know. But it's what I do. And it's not just me. There are others too.' She ran her fingers up and down the stem of the wine glass. 'It's called giving back. I guess in a world of non-stop technology and the search for perfection it's kind of been forgotten along the way.'

He set down his knife and fork and smiled at her. 'You've no idea how good that is to hear.'

She met his gaze and gave a sad kind of smile. 'I sometimes feel as if life is rushing past.' She held out her hand and looked out of the window to the street outside. Even though it was late at night the streets in Temur Sapora were still vibrant with life. The street markets lasted until late in the evening, packed stalls with brightly coloured strips of red and yellow forming the roofs. Business was brisk and the chatter lively.

'I love this place,' she said quietly. 'I love

coming back here.' She took a deep breath then met his watchful gaze. 'But I love my work too.'

'Where are you based now?'

'In Washington. It's great. The team I work with is special. The patients—even more so. I've learned so much.' She kept talking. 'When I come back here I work as a generalist. That's important. I like it. Sometimes, when we specialise, we lose sight of everything else.'

He sat back and looked at her with interest. 'But, when you love something so much, how can you give it up?'

It was the way he said the words, the tiny edge to them that made something inside stand to attention. 'I'm not giving it up,' she said carefully. 'It's still in my heart. I'm just compromising for a few weeks.'

His eyes fixed on his hands on the table. She could tell he was thinking about something else. 'Sometimes we have to do things for other people.' She put her hand on her heart. 'I like that I do that. It keeps me sane. Stops me getting wrapped up in the whirlwind of the world.'

He looked back up to meet her gaze again. Her heart was thudding against her chest. What was it she didn't know about this guy?

It was weird. It was almost as if he had some

kind of aura around him. Something weighing him down.

Her fingers drummed lightly on the table. 'I have to do this. I get so wrapped up in my patients that this is the equivalent of a break for me.' She picked up her napkin and twisted it between her fingers. 'When you're dealing with kids with a potentially terminal condition, it's so easy to let it take over. To search everywhere for the possibility of a new treatment or cure. I get so focused on my work that I forget what else is out there sometimes.'

'Isn't that what everyone wants? A doctor who is committed and dedicated?'

She licked her lips, choosing her words carefully. 'But what if you can't let go? What if you miss something important because you can't see outside your own little box?' She twisted the napkin again. 'I learned a few years ago, to take time to take a breath—to take stock. Some people go skiing. Some people go to the beach—like the resort you were staying at. Some people hire a cabin in the mountains to hide out in. Some people turn off the Internet, the phone and read books.'

A hand reached over and covered hers. She hadn't even realised that her hands were trembling. His warm touch encompassed both of her hands and made her suck in a deep, steadying breath.

Here was she worrying about what he wasn't telling her, but wearing her heart on her sleeve instead. He spoke in a low voice. 'But sometimes you come to a place expecting nothing, and get a whole lot more than you bargained for. Sometimes you don't know what you were looking for until it jumps out and finds you.'

She closed her eyes for a second, her heart rate increasing. Was he talking about work, or something else? It seemed ridiculous to imagine that he could be talking about her—they barely knew each other.

But something was in the air between them. She knew it. And she thought he did too.

He just sat for a few minutes, his hand still over hers. When she opened her eyes again he wasn't staring at her. He was looking at the dark sky outside, his mind obviously someplace else.

Instantly she felt embarrassed, pushing any stray imaginary thoughts aside.

But when Philippe met her gaze he just said simply, 'How about we take a walk? I haven't been on the beach yet in Temur Sapora and I hear it's one of your biggest tourist attractions.'

She was glad of the easy diversion. 'Sure, as a resident it's my duty to show you around.

A walk on the beach at this time of night will be perfect.'

The restaurant was only a few minutes' stroll from the beach. Arissa bent to unfasten her sandals as they got there. He stopped for a few seconds to watch. She grabbed hold of her dress as it fluttered in the ocean wind.

The edge of the beach was lined with thick green foliage. Philippe brushed against some, sending a host of pink butterflies into the dark purple sky. Arissa let out a little yelp, then stood laughing with her hands wide, letting them flutter against her skin.

Philippe stuck his hands into the pockets of his jeans. It was the most relaxed he'd looked since he'd got there. They strolled down next to the rippling ocean. There were a few other couples quietly walking on the beach.

'What happens when you go back?' asked Philippe. 'Do you have someone else lined up to work here?'

She nodded as she kicked at the sand with her bare toes. 'I have a colleague who is a surgeon in Texas. He'll cover the two weeks after I leave.'

'And he'll pick up the research study?'

She bit her bottom lip. 'Yes, well, he should. He's the lead researcher. When the study gets published it will be under his name.'

Philippe stopped walking and turned to face her. 'Why would the study be under his name? I've seen all the files on the computer. This is your study. You made the discovery. You applied for the research ethics and grant. You arranged the protocols. Why on earth wouldn't you publish as the lead researcher?'

She sighed and looked out across the dark ocean. The night sky was littered with sparkling stars, reflecting on the midnight-blue rippling water. She ran her fingers through her hair. She was stalling. She knew that. She wasn't exactly sure how to put this into words.

'This study is going well. It's going better than well. I didn't discover this ointment. It's made from natural products found on Temur Sapora. This ointment was something my grandmother used when I was a child, and her grandmother before her. I just decided to do official research to see how well it actually works.'

'*You* decided,' he emphasised.

She reached up and released her curls from their band, allowing them to fall around her shoulders. 'I just pulled things together. That's all.'

He folded his arms across his chest and moved in front of her, blocking her view of the ocean. The ocean breeze sent his aftershave drifting around her like some sort of protective cloak. His voice was low. 'That's not really an answer. Why don't you want to lead the paper?'

She wrinkled her nose. 'I just...'

'Just?' Now he was smiling, his eyebrows raised. It didn't matter how much she hedged, he wasn't going to let her off with this one.

She sighed again and pointed to the sand. 'Let's sit for a minute.'

He tilted his head to the side and gave her a curious glance then nodded his head. 'Hmm, okay. Let's sit.'

She waited a few seconds until he settled down next to her. She pushed her hand against the cooling sand. It was pressed down hard from the people who'd walked on the beach all day, so she dug her fingers into the sand and pulled some up to run through her fingers.

'So, Dr Arissa Cotter,' he said, 'why on earth wouldn't you want your name on a research paper that's probably going to be widely read, have great acclaim and maybe lead to some money-making opportunities?'

'I don't care about the money,' she said quickly.

He turned his head to face her. 'I might have guessed that already.'

She kept playing with the sand, pressing it between her fingers and letting it grind together. 'The truth is, there's been a whole host of doctors working on this research. The project has lasted around a year. You know that the healing of an ulcer is always a slow process.'

'But not the ulcers you've treated with the ointment,' he said swiftly.

She gave a short laugh. 'Ahh, you've been paying attention. But ulcers we've treated with the placebo—some of them haven't healed at all, so to make a fair comparison I wanted to wait almost a year. I don't want our research to be criticised for short-changing the alternatives.'

'So, the findings are good. Isn't it time to tell the world?'

She nodded her head slowly. 'Yes, it is. But this ointment? It's good. It's *really* good.'

He shook his head again. 'I don't get it. If it was about the money, I could understand you wanting to hold off and get a product licence or patent on the product. But, if it's not about the money, why the delay?'

She pulled a face. 'I don't think this ointment will just do well. I think it will do brilliantly. Just how long has the world waited for something that is more or less guaranteed to heal the biggest chronic leg condition in the world?'

'Exactly. Arissa, what aren't you telling me? Most doctors would be delighted to be part of this research. The prestige you'll get from this alone is amazing.'

She swallowed, her mouth suddenly dry. 'What if I don't want the prestige?' she whispered.

He frowned and reached over to touch her arm. 'What?'

She shook her head. 'I think this research will pretty much explode. There will be conferences and presentations. There will be expectations that I should chat to press about the research and the findings.' She pressed her lips together. 'That's not me. I don't like that. I don't want to be in the public eye.'

He looked stunned. It was the only word to describe the look on his face.

Her stomach was churning. This was personal; it was a bit of herself she didn't like to reveal, but she'd thought he'd understand—chalk it up to anxiety. So many of her friends and colleagues wouldn't dream of being interviewed or standing in front of a room full of people to present research findings. And while that might not be her reason for resisting being lead publisher on the research paper, it was the one she'd fall back on for now.

'That's it?' he queried again.

She nodded. 'There are plenty of other doctors who have worked on this project who would love to be named on the research. I'm happy to step aside. I'm happy to let them deal with all the publicity around it.'

She let out a wry laugh. 'And anyway, my speciality is paediatric oncology, not wound healing.'

But it was clear he wasn't really buying it. 'What you've done here is good. Just about any doctor I know would want to have their name attached to this.'

'Including you?' she snapped. She was getting frustrated now.

He spoke carefully, deep lines appearing on his face as he tried to keep things in check. 'Arissa, this work could be monumental. Headline making.'

'Exactly, and I don't want to make headlines. I'd much rather be in the background.'

It was apparent he didn't understand. 'I just think credit should be given where it is due.'

'Leave it, Philippe.' She was tired. 'I want the research out there. I just don't want to be in the spotlight. I don't want to be in the spotlight at all.'

His face became firm and her stomach flipped a little. For a while it had seemed as if they were about to get to know each other better. The walls around him had come down a bit and she wondered how much more there was to find out about Philippe Aronaz.

But her actions and words had just killed that chance.

She sighed as he stood up and brushed the sand from his trousers. Ever the gentleman, he waited for her to stand up too and put her sandals back on her feet.

The walk home was silent and she blamed herself for the painful awkwardness of it all.

'See you tomorrow?' she said as she finally reached her door. She couldn't help the hopeful tone in her voice.

'Of course.' His answer was perfunctory and delivered with a sharp nod. She watched as he turned and strode down the quiet street.

After a few seconds she rested her head on her door and gave it a half-hearted thump. The guy had given up his holiday to help out at her clinic. He'd offered to help with the research so it didn't fall behind. He didn't need to do any of those things.

He'd taken her to dinner then asked her to go for a walk when it was clear she was still stressed. The guy should be getting nominated for some kind of sainthood. Her?

She'd behaved like Mrs Angry and Mrs Ungrateful. He couldn't possibly understand her feelings because she hadn't wanted to explain.

She didn't feel as if she could. She still couldn't put her finger on it.

Maybe it was the fact she was trying to deny how good-looking and charming he actually was. She was fighting any possible attraction for reasons that only she could understand.

It wasn't wise to mix business with pleasure—even for such a short duration. Plus the fact she still thought there was a lot more beneath the surface of Philippe. There was the distinct impression he wasn't telling her everything she might want to know.

Then, there was the underlying class issue. Money was an issue for her. She knew that people who had money acted differently from the rest of the population. She'd seen it. She'd witnessed it. She didn't need or want to be around anyone that might make her feel 'not good enough' even if it was only in her head.

She sighed and looked up at the dark night sky above, fumbling in her pocket for her key. Every bone in her body ached. Her eyelids were heavy.

She couldn't wait to get to bed.

Tomorrow was another day. She would wake with the intention of making sure Philippe knew she was grateful for his assistance.

It was time to start with a clean slate.

CHAPTER FIVE

PHILIPPE WOKE UP with a growing headache. He wandered over to the glass doors and pulled back the curtains. The turquoise sea was rippling next to the white sand beach decorated by luxury parasols and sunloungers.

He could spend the day there. He could find a book, some sunscreen and lie down for the day, sipping whatever beverage he decided would suit.

It made him want to laugh out loud, because, even with the headache, he knew he would never do it. He rifled through his luggage to find some paracetamol, swallowing them with some water as his concierge showed up with breakfast.

Toast and English breakfast tea. He had decidedly simple tastes.

He glanced at his watch and sat down. It was just past six a.m. His internal body clock just wouldn't let him sleep any longer.

He glanced at his emails, dealing with a few from his father, brother, sister and his personal palace secretary, but, no matter how hard he tried, his thoughts kept drifting back to Arissa and last night.

He'd known that she was overtired. He could tell when she was on edge.

But last night's conversation had gone in a direction he hadn't intended or expected. There had been a real spark of conviction. Determination from Arissa. A real don't-mess-with-me moment.

It set so many alarms pulsing through him.

He was a doctor. He had difficult conversations on a daily basis. He'd always thought he was good at reading signs from his patients. When they were stressed. When they were hiding something. When they were lying.

He'd thought his instincts were normally good. He knew when to push, and when to let something go.

But last night with Arissa it seemed all his usual instincts had flown up into the glittering night sky.

He'd pressed and pressed her when he knew he shouldn't. He just couldn't understand how someone would be part of such an important research project and not want to take any credit for it.

Publishing research was huge in the medical world. Some of his colleagues desperately fought to be involved in studies that they thought could lead to publication and prestige. He'd met people before who genuinely weren't interested in clinical research and just wanted to focus on the job, but he'd never met someone who'd taken part and didn't want to be included in the final result.

It was odd. It was beyond odd. Particularly when, once she had a national platform, she could also use it to talk about the thing that really was true to her heart—the safe haven project. She could find a way to tie the things together. He knew he would.

Her half-hearted explanation of it not being her field hadn't washed with him. Plenty of people changed their speciality or kept an open plan, allowing them to be involved in several projects. It had to be something else—but right now, particularly when he wasn't being entirely honest himself, he didn't feel in a position to push any further.

Arissa appeared to be entirely unique.

But then he'd already thought that when he'd met her.

Philippe had dated plenty of women. You only had to pick up the gossip magazines of Corinez to see the playboy prince tag that wasn't entirely unjustified. He might have gone on a bit of a dating frenzy after the actress fiasco. Whether that was to try and get over his hurt, or just to try and get back out there, he wasn't quite sure. Somehow he had a feeling that if Arissa learned of the playboy prince tag she wouldn't be entirely impressed.

It didn't help that his brother, Anthony, had been dating his wife-to-be for practically his entire life. There was no gossip there—no story. So the press had to concentrate on someone.

He'd spent most of his life in the spotlight. It was part and parcel of being a prince and, although sometimes intrusive, he'd got used to it.

His stomach growled and he quickly ate the toast, dressing as he drank the tea. It was still before seven as he reached the clinic.

His hand hesitated at the handle of the door. What if Arissa was still in a bad mood? What if she was still unhappy with him? He would have to try and make some amends.

As soon as he pushed open the door his nose wrinkled at the smell—the very enticing smell.

Steam was coming from two coffee cups sitting on the table in the staff room, along with a plate of chocolate croissants. It seemed there was a French bakery somewhere in Temur Sapora.

'Oh, you're here.' Arissa halted as she walked

over with another plate in her hands. Her hair was loose around her shoulders and she was wearing a green knee-length shirt dress with a simple tie at the waist. As he moved closer the scent of freesias drifted towards him. He'd noticed it before around her, either her shampoo or her perfume.

'Yes, I'm here,' he said carefully. 'Weren't you expecting me?'

She licked her lips and pushed one of the plates towards him. She seemed nervous. 'Yes, well, I'd hoped you'd still come. Here. I brought a peace offering.'

He tried to hide the smile that wanted to appear as relief flooded through him. 'Why would you need a peace offering?'

She gave a forced kind of smile. 'I think I might have been a bit uptight last night. I thought a visit to our French bakery might stop you deciding to withdraw your services.'

He pulled out a chair and sat down, sliding one of the coffees towards him. 'You thought I would withdraw my services?' Now he truly was surprised.

She gave a half-shrug. 'I might have stayed up half the night worrying about it.'

He shook his head and reached over and squeezed her hand. 'Don't be silly. I'm not going to walk away and leave you on your own.' He raised his eyebrows. 'No matter how cranky you are.'

She mimicked his expression, raising her own eyebrows. 'Cranky?' she queried, grabbing one of the chocolate croissants and ripping it in half, revealing the half-melted chocolate.

He nodded as he took a sip of the coffee. 'Oh, yeah, you're definitely cranky. But, hey, you're stuck with me for the next couple of weeks. I told you. I'm bored.'

He was keeping things simple. If he didn't ask Arissa too many questions, hopefully she would return the favour. It was nice being under the radar for a while and there were benefits to keeping it that way.

The last few months working in one of the hospitals in Corinez had been a different experience from working across the globe. He'd started to take for granted the anonymity of working in other countries. Back home in Corinez everyone knew who he was. Some even addressed him as 'Your Highness'. As much as he wished it wouldn't, it impacted on his work. He'd found things much more difficult back home. But here in Temur Sapora he was regaining the chance of just being Philippe, the regular doctor. Not Philippe, the Prince. And he'd forgotten how much he missed that.

But it seemed that Arissa didn't want to go

into too many details herself. She gave a grateful nod and reached for a laptop. 'I have a way to stop you being bored.'

'You do?' He leaned a little closer.

She pulled up some lists of patients. 'There's a number of patients I'd like to review today—and, if you don't mind, there's a few I'd like you to review too.'

Philippe gave a nod and turned the laptop towards him as he glanced over the list of patients. There was a wide variety. A few of them were on the research study, some had already attended the clinic with chest complaints and been asked to return for review. Another few had minor complaints and required stitches removed.

Philippe gave a smile. Nothing here was arduous. 'No problem. Happy to review all these patients, plus any others that appear at the clinic today.' He glanced at the list that Arissa had prepared for herself. It was full of more children with blood disorders. A completely specialised area that he knew she was best to work on herself.

She leaned her head on her hand and he could see her shoulders visibly relax as she tore off another part of the croissant.

He waited until she'd started chewing before

he spoke again. 'So, I wondered if we could make a trade.'

She stopped chewing and narrowed her gaze suspiciously. 'What kind of trade?'

'A trade for finding out more about the safe haven scheme.'

'You're genuinely interested?'

'Of course I am. You set it up in your country, I want to see if I can set it up in mine.'

The words were out before he really thought about them. 'What country is that, exactly?' she asked.

He pasted on a smile again. 'Just one of the lesser-known Mediterranean countries. It's not well known but near to France, Italy and Monaco.'

She opened her mouth as if she was going to ask him to be more specific but he cut her off quickly. 'Tell me as much as you can before the patients get here.'

The clinic was busy. The weather had been stormy these last few days and it seemed to have irritated just about anyone with a chest condition. She'd spent the morning dealing with kids and adults with asthma, older patients with chronic obstructive pulmonary disease, and a variety of chest infections.

The nurses were triaging the patients as best

they could, and, in the midst of all the chest complaints, they'd had a man with an MI who they'd had to refer on to the hospital, along with a kid with a fractured wrist that required surgery.

She rounded the corner to speak to Philippe about something but stopped as he was bending over a small boy with a lacerated finger. He was speaking quietly but seemed to have really engaged with the child.

'Okay, I'm going to need you to be my really brave champion.' Philippe glanced over his shoulder as if it were a great secret. 'I mean like a superhero.'

The little boy was mesmerised and Philippe started telling him a superhero story to distract him from the stitches. He was finished in a matter of minutes. Then he threw the little boy in the air, declaring him a new champion superhero. They finished with a fist bump and the little boy left the clinic with a wide smile on his face.

She stopped for a second and gave a sigh. It was just another plus point of the guy she was still a bit unsure of.

Philippe was great to work with. No patient was a problem and she trusted his judgement. He seemed to have tireless energy and could last all day on coffee alone. She envied his commitment. And it made her even more curious about him. A guy who could afford to stay at one of the luxury resorts in Temur Sapora was happier slogging his guts out in a community clinic? She couldn't make it up.

But it just made the underlying attraction she felt towards him smoulder even more.

Even watching him from afar was becoming more than a little distracting. He had such a way with the patients, and the few conditions that he came across and was unfamiliar with, he wasn't afraid to come and ask for advice. She liked that. She'd worked with way too many doctors who were arrogant enough never to admit their own lack of knowledge—often to the patient's detriment.

She couldn't quite put her finger on it. There was something about him that wasn't quite off, but just wasn't quite right. Maybe it was her own hang-ups about the rich, the very rich and the very, very rich, that were skewing her normally sound judgement. But whatever it was, the person he was, the *man* he was, was definitely getting under her skin.

Besides the good looks and charm, Philippe Aronaz was, at heart, a good guy. Occasionally he drifted off someplace, as if there was something else on his mind, but most of the time he was focused. He related well to the patients. In fact, it was one of the things that was most impressive about him. He could talk to literally anyone, from cajoling the youngest baby, to having lengthy discussions with some of their most elderly patients. It was almost as if he'd been born to it. And she envied him. She'd had to work hard at that part of herself.

There was always that little part of herself she didn't want to share. She'd shared it once with a colleague at medical school, but the reaction hadn't been good. Her colleague had instantly wanted to do an Internet search on abandoned babies, cross-check with hospital admissions that could be related to childbirth, and search DNA ancestry websites. It almost turned into a personal quest.

They couldn't understand why Arissa didn't want to do all that. They couldn't understand why she wasn't desperate to find out where she came from. Of course, they couldn't begin to realise what it felt like to be abandoned by her mother. To have to spend endless nights wondering if she wasn't good enough, wasn't pretty enough.

Her adoptive parents had told her she was a special angel sent to them from heaven. They'd filled her with such happiness, but told her honestly about her start in life. Arissa had never wanted to be anyone's 'project'. And after that first reaction of sharing her background, she'd learned to keep quiet.

She'd originally lived in one of the smaller villages in Temur Sapora, so no one in the capital city knew her story. No one questioned her dedication to getting the safe haven project off the ground and she'd managed to keep that part of her past out of the public eye. So, trying to connect with patients—opening herself up to people, even just a little—was something she'd struggled with. So, she'd taken steps to stop closing herself off to her patients and their families. Working in paediatric oncology meant she was exposed to a huge amount of joy and pain—she had to be able to have difficult conversations at any point in the day. She had to give people a spark of hope while keeping things realistic. And sometimes she just had to be there, in body and in mind. And she couldn't do that without connecting with people, without exposing a little of herself.

Watching Philippe do things so easily reminded her how hard she'd found her job for a while. It didn't make her resentful. It just made her a little sad that she'd had that experience.

Philippe appeared behind her as she was finishing some notes on a child she'd just seen.

'I phoned to check on the kid yesterday with

the fractured ulna and radius. They had to pin it, but the operation went well.'

'So, no more diving off the rocks and crashing into the sea bed?'

He smiled. 'I think we can safely say his mother will have him bound to some kind of deckchair for the rest of the holiday.'

Arissa pulled a leaflet from the wall. 'I might give the paed ward a call and ask them to steer him towards the community centre. They have less harmful activities for kids during the day that could stop him getting bored.'

Philippe looked over the leaflet and nodded. 'No worries, I'll do it. Nothing worse than a bored, overactive nine-year-old.'

She gave a grateful smile and picked up the list for this afternoon. It was an immunisation clinic and was packed full. Several of the babies had missed some of their routine vaccinations due to coughs, colds and a bout of chicken pox that had been doing the rounds of the local nursery. She put a star at several of the names, taking note that if they didn't show today, she would give them a follow-up call.

'We should break for lunch. Want me to go and grab something?' Philippe asked.

She laughed. 'What—like yesterday?'

Yesterday he'd gone to grab lunch and couldn't make up his mind, coming back with the most bizarre range of foods she'd ever seen—none of which had gone together.

The muffled scream came out of nowhere and they both froze.

Arissa turned, trying to locate where the sound had come from, but Philippe was quicker, heading straight to the front door of the clinic and out onto the street.

She followed him with rapid steps. He stood for a few seconds until he heard the scream again, then moved across the street,

A few people glanced at them. It was a baby crying. Babies cried all the time, but the noise put Arissa's teeth on edge.

Outside the grocery store a tired-looking woman had a small baby on her shoulder, patting its back soothingly.

Arissa recognised her instantly. It was Mariam, one of the local mothers who was due to attend with her baby this afternoon.

She shook her head at Arissa. 'Looks like we won't be getting this immunisation either.' She sighed. 'Rosni has been unsettled all night and she's got a bit of a temperature. Her big brother just had chicken pox. I wonder if she's next.'

The baby screamed again, a high–pitched noise, and Philippe held his hands out straight away, giving Arissa a warning glance. 'Would you mind if I take a look at her?' he said.

When Mariam hesitated he quickly explained. 'I'm one of the doctors that's helping Arissa at the clinic. Dr Aronaz. Do you mind if I take a look at your daughter?'

Mariam's brow creased, instantly worried. 'Do you think there's something wrong?'

Philippe's voice was steady. 'Why don't we just give her a check to be on the safe side?'

Prickles ran down Arissa's spine; she didn't like the sound of the scream any more than Philippe did, but it was clear he had something else on his mind.

She gestured across the road and slid her arm around the woman's waist. 'Come on, Mariam. The clinic's open and there's no one there right now. Let's give Rosni a check and see if she's about to come down with chicken pox.'

Arissa was sure that Philippe wouldn't be reacting like this over a case of chicken pox, but she didn't want to alarm Mariam.

Mariam held out Rosni with slightly shaking hands and Philippe took her quickly and pulled the blanket down that was tucked around her. He gave a nod of his head. 'Let's go over to the clinic.'

It only took a few moments to reach the clinic and set Rosni down on one of the examination tables. Arissa pulled out a tympanic thermometer and pulse oximeter as Philippe gently peeled back Rosni's clothes, speaking to her in a soothing manner.

But Rosni was clearly agitated, her legs and arms flailing wildly and the high-pitched scream continuing.

'Has she fed at all?' he asked Mariam.

Mariam shook her head. 'I tried to feed her all night but she just wasn't interested. I eventually gave her some water this morning—it was all I could get her to take.'

'Have you given her any acetaminophen?'

Mariam shook her head. 'I was just about to buy some. They sell it in the grocery store.'

Philippe continued his examination. When the temperature gauge sounded a few seconds later she turned the screen towards him. The baby's temperature was dangerously high and her heart rate rapid. Rosni continued with the high-pitched wailing as Philippe checked her over. The baby appeared to have bouts of agitation, between periods of sluggishness. Philippe murmured to Arissa, 'Look.' He ran his fingers over the baby's fontanelle. It was bulging slightly.

She started and walked quickly over to one of the locked clinic cupboards. She grabbed some IV antibiotics, some acetaminophen, and some other equipment from the cupboards.

Philippe narrowed his gaze in question. He

was still examining Rosni, checking the palms of her hands, soles of her feet and eyes. There was no obvious rash right now, but sometimes in Malaysian children rashes could be difficult to spot. He shook his head.

Mariam was getting more anxious by the minute. 'What's wrong with my baby?'

Arissa gave Philippe a quick nod of her head. It didn't matter that this was her clinic. She'd never had a child with meningitis before and it was clear that Philippe had got this.

He bent to speak to Mariam. 'We have to act quickly, Mariam. I think Rosni might have meningococcal meningitis. I can see from her chart she's had her first vaccination but not the rest.'

'She's been sick. There hasn't been time…'

Philippe put his hand on Mariam's shoulder. 'This isn't your fault. We don't normally see meningitis in babies as young as Rosni. She's just unlucky.'

'You're sure that's what it is?' Mariam's voice was trembling.

He gave a sorry nod. 'I've heard this scream only once before.'

Arissa stepped up alongside him. 'It's important we give Rosni antibiotics as soon as possible. We have them here—for emergency circumstances like these.'

'Shouldn't she go to hospital?'

Arissa nodded. 'Yes, absolutely. But if we call an ambulance now it will still be over an hour before you reach the hospital. We'll start the antibiotics now before we call the ambulance.'

Philippe picked Rosni up and put her on the baby scale for a second, taking a quick note of her weight. It only took a few moments to work out how much of the medicines to give the baby and Philippe found a tiny vein quickly to slide in an IV portal. 'Just as well you've got these,' he said quietly as Arissa bent beside him to assist.

She gave a brief nod. 'Let's just say we've learned over the years to plan for every contingency.' Her shirt was sticking to her back and she gave an uncomfortable shudder. 'But I'm glad I've never had to do this before.'

His hand closed over hers for a few seconds as she passed over the syringe with the antibiotics. His eyes turned to the clock to begin the administration. 'Hopefully this is a one-off,' he said. 'You call the ambulance, then I guess we'll spend the rest of the day contact tracing.'

She sucked in a breath. She hadn't even thought of that. Of course.

She couldn't help but admire how smoothly he'd handled all this. It was likely she would have gone outside to see whose baby had been crying like that—but would she have recognised the signs of meningitis as quickly as Philippe had?

As an ER doc it was likely he'd had cases before. Any case she'd dealt with in paediatrics had already been diagnosed, or been under investigation, by the time they'd got to her. She'd had to perform lumbar punctures to guarantee a diagnosis on small children before, but most of the initial diagnostics had already been recognised.

Arissa made the call for the ambulance, then phoned the referral through to the hospital so they would be ready to expect the patient. She then grabbed a chart to make some notes and went back to Mariam. 'I know you also have a son, Mariam. Are there any other children in the house?'

She shook her head. 'Just my son, Vasan. He's three.'

Arissa took a quick note. 'I'll arrange for some oral antibiotics for your son. Anyone else in the household? Or has Rosni been at nursery?' She tried to be as methodical as possible, taking all the notes she should to ensure that anyone potentially exposed to meningitis would be identified and protected.

Philippe continued the slow and steady administration of the antibiotic, monitoring the baby for any reaction. Rosni was still agitated—the medications taking time to take effect. The ambulance arrived around fifteen minutes later, the paramedic more than capable of dealing with their charge.

By the time the ambulance left Arissa was exhausted. She slumped against the door jamb and took a deep breath.

Philippe sat down at one of the tables and put his head in his hands. She realised instantly he was upset, much more than his calm demeanour had implied. She walked over and, after hesitating for a second, sat down at right angles to him, close enough to touch him.

She reached up her hand, holding it just next to his hand before changing her mind and edging her seat closer. She took both his hands in hers and lowered them to the table. His head was still bowed. So, she took a deep breath and lowered her head so her forehead was against his.

His voice was low, throaty. 'Once you hear the cry you never forget it.'

His breath was warm next to her skin. She could see the faintest tremble in his hands. She licked her lips slowly then asked the question. 'When did you hear the cry before?'

He shivered. His eyes still closed. 'A few

years ago in another ER. I'd just come on shift. The woman had been in the waiting room for a few hours.'

Arissa's stomach sank. From his reaction she could almost guess what might have happened. 'How did that baby do?'

He clenched her fingers tightly. 'He made it—but barely. His vaccinations were up to date, but his mum had put him to bed and given him some acetaminophen when he'd developed a fever. She'd brought him in to the ER in the middle of the night when he hadn't settled.'

'And she was still waiting when you came on duty?'

He nodded and winced. 'There had been a road traffic accident, and a house fire. No one had a chance to properly assess the baby.'

She squeezed his hands. 'But you did.'

He shook his head slightly. 'It was almost too late. The baby fitted within a few minutes. It was a few days before we knew if the baby would live or die.' He licked his lips. 'The baby recovered, but there were some long-term effects. He lost his hearing. If I'd got to him quicker…' His voice trailed off.

He stopped talking, his eyes closing again. It was the first time she'd ever seen him shaken. How much had it taken for him to hold things together while Mariam and her baby had been here?

She took a deep breath. 'I'm really sorry to hear about that baby, to hear about how busy the ER was. I'm sorry for him, and the fact that he lost his hearing.' She sucked in another breath. 'But, Philippe, I'm not sorry you heard the cry. I'm not sorry that today you recognised the cry instantly and acted appropriately. If I'd been on my own, it might have taken me a bit longer to reach the diagnosis, and we both know that time is of the essence.' She pulled one of her hands free of his and reached up and touched his cheek. 'You did good today, Philippe. You've probably saved Rosni's life—and the rest of the family that's been exposed.'

He opened his eyes, his lashes only an inch from hers. His dark eyes were so deep, so full of emotion that she blinked back tears. 'You did good today, Philippe. Don't forget that. We all have cases we can't ever forget.'

It was odd. She'd never expected to get so up close and personal with this man who was still a bit of a mystery to her. But this just felt so right. He was her colleague. He was helping her. He had likely just saved a baby's life and that had obviously brought back some hidden memories.

She gave him the smallest smile. 'Thank

you,' she whispered. 'You made a difference today. That's all we can ever ask.'

And they sat there, foreheads touching, until the first patient arrived for the vaccination clinic.

CHAPTER SIX

He was unsettled. If he tried to be rational about things he would put it down to the baby conjuring a wave of memories and emotions and the frustration he'd felt first time around.

But it wasn't the baby. He'd checked on Rosni, and after a few days in hospital she'd made a good recovery thanks to the early administration of antibiotics. None of the other family members or kids at nursery had developed symptoms. So, he should be happy. But he wasn't. He couldn't think straight.

Maybe it was the pressure of the job awaiting him back home. Maybe it was the million and one ideas that were clamouring for space in his head about how he could reform health services in Corinez. He had to start somewhere. His head was swimming. So many things needed to change back home.

But the truth was he knew exactly what was unsettling him. The days were marching on in Temur Sapora and his relationship with Arissa was growing every day. They worked well together, almost anticipating each other's requests, and at the end of each day, they sat down together, debriefed, then generally spent the evening in each other's company.

Sometimes it was dinner in a local restaurant, other times they grabbed a takeaway. Sometimes it was just a walk around the streets or down to the beach. But the more time he spent with the quietly gorgeous, unassuming doctor, the more time he wanted to spend with her. And she still didn't know who he was.

The thing that had initially just been a vague and unimportant secret was beginning to feel like the elephant in the room. Why hadn't he just told her straight away who he was? Now, it felt as if he were deliberately lying to her.

No one had recognised him in Temur Sapora and, for that, he was eternally grateful. But every day he was cautious, quickly checking the Internet for any mentions. It was almost like being off the grid and that had entirely been his intention when he'd come here. But now his intention seemed a little…deceitful.

Part of him was grateful for the chance just to be 'Philippe'. No Prince. No Royal Highness. No one treating him differently at work. No actress waiting on the sidelines. *My Night with the Charming Prince* had been the headline after the interview.

But how would Arissa feel about headlines like that?

As he finished scrubbing his hands in the sink, she appeared at the edge of the door. 'Almost done?'

He nodded. They'd finished work for the day and made plans for dinner. For the first time he was going to see the inside of her home as Arissa had offered to teach him to cook some traditional Malaysian dishes.

Her curls were loose and bouncing on her shoulders, she was wearing flat shoes and a red shirt dress that complemented her skin tone and dark eyes.

He gave a quick nod. 'Let me change my shirt. I brought another with me.' She raised her eyebrows and smiled as he strode towards the staff room. His cream short-sleeved shirt and jeans were sitting in the corner along with his antiperspirant and aftershave. Two minutes later he was ready and stood next to her as she locked up the clinic.

'It was a good day today,' she murmured.

'It was,' he agreed. The research study results were remarkable. He'd seen a patient today whose leg ulcer had almost completely healed in a few short weeks—a leg ulcer that he'd had for more than four years. The ointment really was working wonders.

Arissa's hand brushed against his as they walked down the main street. 'I've still not heard from the professor of my new hospital,' she said absent-mindedly.

'Isn't it less than a week until you go?'

She nodded. 'I fly out on Sunday. I've filled in endless amounts of paperwork for the recruitment agency and the hospital HR people. It doesn't usually take this long to sort out. I've had a deposit down on my accommodation for the last four months.'

They crossed into the nearby grocery store. Arissa had already pre-ordered supplies so Philippe just paid for them and carried the brown bag. 'Maybe it's just an administration thing. Some places aren't as organised as others. Have you tried to call them?'

She gave a shrug. 'Only about a dozen times. No one seems to answer their phones. I sent another email today though. If I don't get a reply I'll try again tomorrow.'

They turned down a street that ran parallel to the beach. It was lined with small bungalows painted in a variety of colours. Arissa stopped outside a pale yellow one and pulled the keys from her pocket.

'This is a fantastic location,' enthused

Philippe. 'You're only a few steps from the beach.'

Arissa nodded. 'Yeah. I love it. This was my parents' house and my grandparents' before that. Most of the houses in this row are generational properties.'

He looked around the bungalow as he stepped inside. From the outside there were two large windows at the front. One was in the main room, which was small but contained a comfortable sofa that gave a great view of the beach, and the back of the room opened out into the kitchen with a small dining table.

Arissa waved over to the left. 'My bedroom and the bathroom are over that side. There's another room that's literally just a broom cupboard. That used to be my bedroom, but I use it as a study now.'

'You never wanted to move?'

She waved a hand towards the view. 'Who wouldn't want to live on the beach? My mum and dad could have moved to a bigger house a number of times over the years, but the beach and the view kept them here.'

Philippe walked over to a framed photo on the wall. It showed a much younger Arissa, between an older man and woman who were both beaming down at her with their arms around her shoulders.

He asked the inevitable question. 'Where are they now?'

She moved towards him, holding out her hands for the brown paper bag. 'Let's just say I was a late—but much-wanted—baby. My mother died of breast cancer a few years ago, and my father had an accident when he was out on one of the fishing boats a few months later.'

'I'm so sorry.'

She gave the briefest nod of her head; one hand reached up and traced over the figures in the photo for a second. 'I was lucky to have them as long as I did. They were proud of me. Saw me through medical school, and they were the proudest parents in the room at my graduation.' He could see the love on her face, the admiration for two people that at one point had been her whole world.

He watched her for a few moments as he realised how big this was for her. She'd invited him back to her house, to see a part of her that most people wouldn't know. It made the fact he'd been less than straightforward with her rest heavily on his shoulders.

She took the bag and carried it over to the small kitchen. Philippe moved beside her. 'So, you've never wanted to sell up, even though you don't stay here permanently?' He was curious. She only got to spend around six weeks a year here, and he could imagine that over the years this small bungalow had become prime property.

She shook her head. 'Absolutely not. I sometimes rent the place out to some of the visiting doctors—but only if I know them. Otherwise, I just look forward to getting back here five or six weeks a year.'

He turned and took another glance at the view. A burst of yellow sand, followed by endless turquoise ocean. It really was a prime view. The beach was sheltered, in a little inlet, with no other property overlooking it. 'I can imagine you've had offers for a place like this.'

She nodded as she emptied the chicken, noodles, herbs and spices out onto the counter. 'From the developers? Constantly. Particularly since we own not just the bungalows, but the beach too. But the rest of the people in the street feel the same as I do. Staying here is like a family tradition to me. I get to call this piece of paradise mine.' She put one hand up to her chest. 'I might not be here all year round, but it's here whenever I need it.' She met his gaze with her dark brown eyes. 'You can't sell a part of yourself.'

There it was. The connection. It practically zinged in the air between them. Arissa could probably make a fortune if she sold up and moved. But her heart was here. He could see that. She was grounded here. Even though her family were gone. She loved her island—just as he loved his country.

Nowadays so many people were indifferent about where they stayed—flitting about from place to place, prioritising money over so much else. It was refreshing to meet someone who had as much commitment to their home as he did.

'Family traditions are very important where I come from too,' he said softly. He should tell her. He should tell her now about who he really was. But he didn't want to spoil this moment or time between them.

This was the closest he'd felt to someone in, well, for ever. She didn't know him as a prince. She didn't want anything from him, and he liked holding onto that thought. That feeling.

She blinked and licked her lips, before lowering her eyes as she rearranged the ingredients. 'You're the first man I've invited back here in years,' she said slowly.

The air around them seemed heavy. Every breath a little more laboured than the one before. There was a slight tremble in her hands. She was nervous. He was making her nervous.

But somehow he knew it wasn't a bad nervous. Because he felt exactly the same.

'I'm honoured to be here,' he said simply as one of his hands moved over hers. 'Thank you for inviting me.' The touch of her warm skin against his sent a little buzz up his skin. He liked it. He liked it a lot.

The aroma of freesias drifted towards him. Perfume. She'd put on perfume when he'd changed. His heartbeat quickened.

He wanted to move closer. To slip his hands around her waist and turn her towards him. But it seemed too forward. Too presumptuous.

Arissa's hand moved from under his and she stepped to one side, giving him a smile over her shoulder. Was she deliberately putting a little distance between them?

He wasn't sure. But what he was sure about was that he didn't want to put a foot wrong. He didn't want to step anywhere she didn't want him. She pulled out a wok and sat it on the hotplate. 'Okay, before we start, no allergies?'

He shook his head; he was happy to take her lead. He'd agreed to make her dinner. That was exactly what he would do. 'No allergies, why?'

She grinned. 'Because I like peanuts with my chicken.'

He wrinkled his nose. 'Peanuts?'

She nodded and pointed towards the chopping board and knives. 'Peanuts. Okay, grab your tools and let's get started. I'm famished.'

He looked at the array of ingredients in front of him. He wasn't quite sure where to start, but the chicken seemed like a safe bet so he started chopping that.

'What are you teaching me?' he asked. 'What recipe are we creating?'

She opened a cupboard and lifted out two wine glasses, taking a bottle from the fridge. 'I'm teaching you how to make Malaysian spicy chicken noodles.' She poured the wine. 'But I want you to know that I have an unusual way of teaching.' She took a sip from her wine glass and winked at him.

A smile automatically came to his lips. She was flirting with him, always a good sign. 'What's unusual about your teaching methods?'

She let out a laugh. 'I don't actually do anything. I just watch you do it. I'm like the ultimate lazy tutor.'

He moved from chopping the chicken, to shredding the cabbage and carrots, all the while feeling her gaze on him. He might be a prince, but he'd learned to fend for himself over the years. He wasn't above throwing some ingredients together. And somehow he liked being under her appreciative gaze.

She nodded towards the sesame oil next to the wok and smiled. 'Better get started.' It was as if her gaze was dancing across his skin, leaving tension in the air between them, and he'd never liked it so much.

He shook his head and poured some oil into the already smoking wok, watching while it spat instantly. He added the chicken, the vegetables and some of the baby bok choy, chilli paste, garlic, soy sauce and finally some hokkien noodles. Last thing he wanted to do was mess up dinner.

'Wait!' Arissa smiled. 'You've forgotten my favourites.'

She grabbed a packet of peanuts and sprinkled them over the dish.

He gave a little frown. 'Are you sure these are a good match?'

She raised her eyebrows knowingly as she put out two place settings. 'These are my secret ingredient.'

He dished out the stir-fry into the two white bowls she'd set next to him and carried them over to the table. 'Do I get to drink my wine now?'

She nodded as he sat down opposite her and he lifted his glass to hers. 'To friends,' he said. 'You've made this holiday a whole lot more…' he wasn't quite sure what word to add—what word would be entirely appropriate '…special,' finished with a broad smile.

She clinked her glass against his. 'Special,' she repeated as her gaze connected with his. 'To think I could have spent two weeks entirely on my own.' She took a slow breath, as she held his gaze. 'I'm glad you're here.'

'Me too.'

They ate as the sun set on the horizon sending streaks of orange and red across the sky. When they finished they carried their glasses outside and sat on the cooling sand on the beach.

'Last time around you didn't tell me you owned a whole beach,' he joked.

'Last time around I didn't know you that well,' she replied. 'And I don't own the whole beach.' She drew a little square in the sand between them. 'Maybe just, this much.'

He didn't hesitate, he closed his hand over hers, guiding a finger to draw a wider square. 'Or maybe you own a little more. This much?'

She laughed and lay back on the sand. 'Heard of snow angels? How about some sand angels?' She was still smiling; she started swishing her arms and legs over the sand. 'Maybe it's this much.'

He moved over slightly, lying back too and copying her actions. 'Or maybe it's this much!'

She kept laughing as she watched him. He

finally stopped and turned around onto his side, putting his head on one hand.

'We have a whole beach to ourselves,' he said conspiratorially. 'Any ideas what to do next?'

She turned to face him, putting her head on her hand too and shaking some sand from her hair as he eyed the rippling ocean.

'No way,' she said firmly.

'Why not?' He couldn't hide the gleam in his eyes and sat up straight. 'Come on.' He pulled his shirt over his head.

She burst out laughing and he looked down and held out his hands. 'What? Too much paunch?' He knew he looked fine; his almost washboard abs had been gained through long hours at work, not long hours in the gym.

She shook her head. 'There's no paunch—' she wagged her finger '—but don't go any further.'

'Why not?' He was being wicked and he knew it. He unfastened his jeans and laughed as she put one hand up to her face and looked away. 'Somehow as a doc, I think you've seen it all before.'

He kicked his jeans off and held out his hand towards her. 'You're telling me, in all the years you've stayed here, you've never gone skinny-dipping in the ocean?'

Her eyes widened. 'Not with anyone watching. Anyhow—' she sat up onto her knees '—I normally use a bathing suit—don't most people?'

He winked as he looked down at his jersey boxer shorts. 'Depends on the occasion.' He checked over his shoulder. The beach was empty and the sun was dipping even lower in the sky, the rainbow of reds and oranges vivid in the dimming light.

'Thought you were introducing me to Temur Sapora,' he teased, his arm still outstretched and not wavering at all.

Her fingers went to the top button on her shirt dress as she started to stand. The little flicker in his stomach grew.

She undid the first button. 'I'm introducing you to *selected* portions of Temur Sapora. Maybe I hadn't decided if you were worthy of this yet?' She was teasing him back. He liked it.

She still hadn't taken his hand. He stepped a little closer. 'What do I need to do to be worthy?' he asked, his voice low.

She blinked, those dark eyes connecting with his. It was mesmerising watching her fingers oh-so-slowly undoing the buttons on her dress, revealing the skin underneath. His breath was definitely faltering.

The red dress dropped to her feet in silence. Her underwear was simple. Black cotton bra and pants. No silk. No lace. He'd never seen anything sexier.

There was a glint in her eye. She pointed over his shoulder. 'See that buoy out there?'

He turned. The orange buoy was bouncing in the currents. He looked sideways at her, knowing what might come next. 'Yes...'

She streaked past him. 'Last one there's the loser!'

He couldn't help but admire her curvy figure as she ran full pelt into the waves—the actions of someone who'd done it time and time before. She hit the water with her arms automatically starting to crawl as he was still standing on the beach.

Her swimming was smooth and practised, and it gave him the kick he needed to run and join her. Philippe had always had a competitive edge but this was one contest he was definitely prepared to lose.

He waded through the ocean, sucking in a breath at how deceptively cold it was at first, then put his head down and started out towards the buoy. Arissa was already halfway there.

He kicked his legs more, his arms slicing through the ocean. Every so often he lifted his head to check the position of both Arissa and the buoy. Her laugh carried over the water towards him. He was catching her, but it was clear she was confident.

He slowed his pace a little. She was relaxing around him, flirting a little and he liked it. He liked her. She was interesting, clearly dedicated to her work and home, but there was real old-fashioned goodness about her that he hadn't seen in years. And it was in everything that she did. Every conversation. Every thought process.

Nowadays, if he said that, it probably wouldn't be seen as a compliment. But he admired how much the people around her mattered to her, because it was exactly how he felt when he was at home too.

So many people were interested in fame and fortune now. Social media and press seemed to dictate even diplomatic processes and business dealings. It wasn't that he was wildly old-fashioned, but he'd become a doctor for a reason—because he liked to deal with *people*.

Nowadays it sometimes felt as if it was turning into an original concept.

She let out a whoop and he looked up to see her laughing and touching the buoy. He was only a few strokes behind and joined her holding onto the bright orange float. 'Cheater.' He laughed as he spat out some water.

'Not at all.' She grinned. 'If you're not fast, you're last.'

He ducked her head under the water and she came up spluttering but still laughing. This time she moved closer, one arm sliding around his neck as she used him as her anchor instead of the buoy.

'Maybe you just need to learn to swim better,' she taunted, her legs wrapping around his waist.

For the first time he was glad of exactly how cold this water was. Not that it was stopping his blood flowing.

'Maybe you've had more practice.' He smiled back. 'Given that you've got your own private beach.'

She tipped her head back, letting some of the water drain from her hair, the curls were still there, just bouncier now. He tried not to stare at the delicate skin on her neck and the base of her throat. It would only lead his eyes to someplace else.

As she tipped her head back up her grin was wide, showing her straight white teeth. 'Is that beach envy I hear in your voice, Dr Aronaz?' She was still teasing. He liked this new side of her. It seemed as if once she'd shed her clothes, she'd also managed to shed that serious cloud that seemed to hang around her. He still hadn't quite got to the bottom of that.

She leaned forward, her lips brushing against

the edge of his cheek. 'One more race, then. First back to the beach.'

He froze, still in place in the water; between the feel of her lips on his cheek and the press of her breasts against his chest as she did that, he'd pretty much lost the ability to concentrate at all.

She let go quickly, turning in the water and heading back to shore. He took a few moments, watching her go. When was the last time this had happened to him?

He'd dated plenty of women—he hadn't picked up the title of Playboy Prince for nothing—but he'd never dated anyone that clean took his breath away. He'd just never thought that was possible. More like an old wives' tale that people liked to mention to pretend just 'how in love' they were with their spouse or current partner.

He'd never really believed those sensations actually existed. But here, right in the middle of the cold South China Sea, he'd just had an awakening. He'd learned something new.

And he didn't know quite what to do with it.

She was slicing through the waves like a mermaid and it brought him to his senses. He crawled lazily along behind, no chance of catching up, while his brain churned with a whole host of new emotions.

Philippe Aronaz wasn't used to being wrong-footed. He was always in control.

He watched as Arissa waded out of the water and turned to watch him, shaking her head with her hands on her hips. She picked up the red dress and held it in front of her as he waded out behind her and walked across the sand.

He was conscious of every bead of water dripping from his skin—just as he was conscious of the rivulets of water running down the length of her. 'Come on.' She nodded back towards the bungalow. 'I'll get you a towel.'

She turned and started walking towards the pale yellow house. He was slow to pick up his shirt and jeans as he watched her retreating form dressed only in her underwear.

His mind could go so many places right now. And to be honest, he wanted it to. But deep down, his internal voice was screaming at him. *Don't take things for granted. Don't move too soon.*

Arissa Cotter was special. He didn't want to assume anything. Just because she'd let her guard down a little tonight, and just because she'd moved next to him—touched him—didn't mean anything.

Somehow he wanted to do everything right around her.

He walked slowly back to her house. She met

him at the door with a big blue fluffy towel that she thrust towards him. 'Dry off in there.' She gestured towards her bathroom, before disappearing into her bedroom with a towel of her own.

His body almost let out a growl. But he shook his head and took himself into the bathroom, drying off and re-dressing—even though it was the last thing he wanted to do.

By the time he emerged, Arissa was standing in the middle of her living room, dressed in a baggy green T-shirt and jersey shorts. Her hair was still damp and curled around her shoulders.

'Okay?' she asked.

'Of course,' seemed the natural reply. All of a sudden a wave of awkwardness swept over him. He could say something. He could ask the question. He could ask her what she wanted to happen next. But in the dim light of her bungalow, and the small space of her living room, it didn't seem quite right. It almost felt a bit intrusive, and the last thing he wanted her to feel was any pressure.

'Thank you for tonight,' he said softly. 'I had a great time.' He took a few steps towards the door.

'I did too.' Her reply was so quiet he almost didn't hear it, his hand already on the doorknob. He pulled it open. The sun had finally vanished leaving the semi-dark sky sprinkled with glistening white stars.

As he turned back she'd moved right behind him.

He could have stopped. He could have said something clever. But instead he let his instincts take over and he bent, capturing the back of her head in his hands, letting his fingers slide through her damp curls and tugging her mouth towards his.

They both tasted of the ocean, both still smelling of the tang of the sea. But the scent was heady, wrapping around them as her hands slid up around his neck.

She didn't object, her kiss matching his in every way.

His brain was soaring. He wanted more. But he knew right now that he had to step away.

He kept his hands at her head, forcing himself not to move them to her body, but instead bringing one around to the side of her cheek. When their kissing finally slowed he pulled back and licked his lips, catching his breath slowly.

Her cheeks were slightly flushed, her eyes wide, but she didn't make any further move either, just watching him carefully.

He smiled at her and stepped back. 'Goodnight, Arissa,' he said hoarsely.

She gave a little nod of her head. 'Goodnight, Philippe,' she replied. There was a smile on her lips, as if she too was trying to take stock of what had just happened between them.

He turned and headed back down the street, willing himself not to look back, and feeling the blood pulsing through his veins. He couldn't work out if he was crazy, composed, or contrite.

He'd wanted more, but stepping away had been the only truthful thing he could do. She didn't know everything about him yet. He needed to have that conversation, and it wasn't one you had when your arms were wrapped around someone, either in the water or out.

He sighed and looked up at the dark night sky, shaking his head at himself. First day on this island had seemed so long. Now, two weeks seemed as if they would never possibly be long enough.

CHAPTER SEVEN

THE NEXT FEW days were a mixture of easy and frustrating.

It was clear that neither of them could forget that kiss.

She'd wondered if things would be slightly awkward between them, but that first morning after, when she'd walked into the clinic, he'd already been there—with coffee and croissants—and he'd just shot her that sexy grin through tired eyes and gestured to the seat beside him. 'I started early.'

So had she. In fact she hadn't slept a wink after that kiss, wondering if she should just have grabbed him by his shirt collar and dragged him back into her house. Instead, she'd slid down the inside of her door once she'd closed it—her legs like jelly, smiling away to herself. It would be so easy to blame the unexpected swim, but she'd known the jelly legs were entirely down to Philippe.

The croissant and coffee had settled her jittering nerves. And Philippe had been entirely *normal*. Not ignore-the-fact-it-happened normal. No, he'd continued to let his hand linger when they touched, she'd occasionally caught him watching her with his sexy smile, but all the while entirely being a gentleman around her.

She wasn't sure whether to laugh or cry.

There was something so nice about being around him, laughing with him, talking with him. For such a long time she'd been on her own. Between her commitments to home and her commitments to work, she really hadn't had time in her life for anyone else. Philippe made things easy. She didn't need to try. She didn't need to worry about what she was wearing, or how her hair looked, or whether she'd remembered to put make-up on that day.

They'd had lunch and dinner together every day and evening. They hadn't had a second performance of that night-time swim—or of the kiss—but it was weird. She could almost swear that at times the air between them sparkled.

How stupid was that? An entirely rational, educated woman who thought the air might sparkle between her and some guy? It was like flitting back into her eight-year-old self when she'd imagined she'd marry a prince, and ride off on the back of a unicorn across a rainbow, all while the air around her glimmered. Of course at that point, in her dream she hadn't been wearing a princess dress, she'd been wearing a NASA space suit because her intention had been to be an astronaut. Ridiculous.

Part of her knew that Philippe was only here for another few days. To expect anything other than a fleeting friendship would be ridiculous. But other parts of her felt as if this was some old-fashioned kind of courtship. And she couldn't pretend that didn't warm her heart entirely.

She gave a smile and called her last patient into the second vaccination clinic of the week. There was a queue of patients—Philippe had seen half of the children and the time had flown past. He gave a nod as she escorted the mother and baby into her room. 'I'll put the kettle on,' he mouthed before following it with a cheeky wink.

Her heart scattered across her chest and she hid the smile as she focused on her patient. 'Welcome, Ana, it's lovely to see you again.'

He folded his arms as the coffee percolated. He could have gone out to buy some from across the street but that would only have killed time and he couldn't put this off any longer. He had to tell Arissa who he really was.

His stomach was churning. His two weeks were rapidly coming to an end. He knew that he'd be heading off on the plane soon, what he didn't know was whether he'd have a chance to pursue this blossoming relationship with Arissa.

It surprised him just how much he wanted to. Just how important this was to him. They were right at the beginning. Who knew where this could lead? But with him in Corinez, and her heading to the UK, there would be hundreds of miles between them. Could a long-distance relationship actually work? Particularly when they were both so dedicated to their jobs? All he knew for certain was that he wanted to try.

He waited as she saw the last patient out of the clinic and closed the door for lunch.

But before he had a chance to speak she stopped at the computer to check her emails.

Her face fell.

'What's wrong?' he couldn't help but ask.

She was staring at the screen, then shook her head for a few moments and picked up her phone. 'Give me a minute, would you?'

The expression on her face was a mixture of panic and worry. She disappeared into the office with her phone pressed to her ear. The door didn't entirely close.

He paced around outside. Attempting to be busy doing other things and trying his best not to listen, but it was hard not to hear the rising tones of her voice.

After around fifteen minutes she appeared at the doorway, her face drawn.

'What is it, Arissa?' He couldn't help himself. He walked over and put his hands on her arms.

She shook her head. She looked numb. 'There's been a problem with my visa. The agency I'm due to start with in London hasn't applied in time. I needed the visa to secure my post in London at the children's hospital.'

Philippe frowned. Doctors moved to positions in other countries all the time. Visas were always a tricky issue, but usually dealt with promptly and without delay when the paperwork was submitted. 'Have they made a mistake?'

She nodded. 'Oh, yes.'

'Can the hospital sort it out for you?'

She gulped and shook her head. For the first time he thought he could see tears glistening in her eyes. 'No. It's too late. They need someone to start August the first. My visa will never process in time. It was part of the terms and conditions of the contracts that the visa requirement would be met by a certain time. They can't afford to leave posts like this vacant, Philippe. These kids need doctors. They don't have time for delays.' Her voice was shaking now.

Philippe could see the pain in her eyes. 'But they need you. They'll be able to pull some strings. Doctors are a priority around the world. If we can speak to the visa office, I'm sure they'll sort things out for you.'

She shook her head again. 'They won't buy it. As soon as the hospital were notified my paperwork wasn't agreed in time, they offered the post to someone else.'

She sagged down into a chair. 'For the first time in my life—I don't have a job to go to.'

He could see how upset she was by this. He was upset for her. Most doctors were meticulous planners. They all knew that job visa requirements could take months and generally worked with agencies to ensure all these things were in order well in advance.

He knew how hard she'd been working. Covering the job she'd had in Washington, spending all her holiday time here, and helping document the research. It was no wonder something had slipped. It could happen to the best of people.

But from the look on her face it had never happened to Arissa before.

'I can try and help. Let me see what I can do. Let me try and speak to someone.' He was babbling now and he knew it.

But she shook her head again. Her eyes were vacant when they met with his. 'But the job's gone already. Even if strings were pulled and I got my visa, I wouldn't get this job. The opportunity is gone.'

It was almost as if all the energy had gone from her body. Her shoulders sagged, her head dipped and her breathing got heavier.

He'd never seen her like this.

His mind was whirling around and around. He knew exactly what he should do right now. But the timing just felt so off.

It was inevitable. He'd spent the last two weeks in a bubble that didn't really exist. It was time to tell the truth. His brain was desperately trying to create a spin on what he was about to reveal.

He took a deep breath. 'Arissa, I know this is a shock. But, maybe this means you have an opportunity to do something different?'

'Different like what? What else is there that I can possibly do?'

He gave her a hesitant smile. 'How about I take you someplace else? A different country. A country that could benefit from your expertise.'

She frowned and shook her head. 'What?'

It was clear she had no idea where this was heading.

There were parts of this story that he knew she wouldn't be happy about. He took a few breaths. 'Arissa, have you heard of Corinez?'

She shook her head. 'Where?'

He wasn't offended. While most people in Europe had heard of Corinez, in other continents around the world it wasn't so well known.

'Corinez. It's an island near France, Monaco and Italy.'

A frown creased her brow. 'Corinez? That's the place you're from?'

He nodded. 'I'm due to go back—to start a new job…' he cringed as he said those words '… and I wonder if—until you get things sorted—you would come with me.'

For a few seconds she looked stunned, then confused. The frown in her brow grew even deeper. 'To do what?'

He paused for a moment. 'I have a senior position. One that means I'd be able to look at the possibility of setting up a scheme similar to the safe haven scheme you've set up here.'

It didn't take more than a few seconds for the pieces to fall into place for Arissa. It wasn't usual for a doctor who'd spent the last few years specialising in an ER to go to a job like that. 'Exactly what kind of job do you have in Corinez?'

'I'm part of an advisory committee.' He kept his reply short.

Her eyes widened. 'An advisory committee for a hospital?'

He hesitated. 'No…an advisory committee for the whole country.'

'Wow. That sounds important.' She gave a little smile. 'I don't mean to be cheeky, but how on earth would you get a job like that?'

He looked up and met her confused gaze. 'I was born into it.'

He waited. She pulled back. 'What on earth does that mean?'

'It means that I was born to be on the advisory committee for overseeing healthcare. My sister was born to do the same for finance, and my brother…' he took another breath '…he was born to be King.'

Silence. So long and so amplified that the breath he was holding almost burst his lungs.

She seemed frozen. Her eyes couldn't get any wider. Finally, she made a kind of stuttering sound. 'So…so…if your brother will be King…that makes you a prince?'

He flinched at the way she said the word—as if it were some kind of awful disease.

He nodded. His heart heavy. Most of his life

when he'd dated he'd wondered if people were going out with him *because* he was a prince, not because he was Philippe. Working in the hospital in Corinez had felt almost awkward. People had been ridiculously polite to him, tiptoeing around him when they should have been more worried about providing healthcare.

But coming here had been something again. He'd never had such a blank slate before. And for the first time he'd managed to have a friendship develop and blossom with no underlying knowledge of his true identity. For his part, it wasn't exactly honest—he knew that. But it had felt so freeing—even if it was only a few days.

He knew that the start of the friendship between him and Arissa had been about him. About them.

'Why didn't you tell me?' Her voice was tight.

He ran his hand through his hair. 'Because I came here under the radar, for a holiday. I met Dr Reacher on the plane. When he told me what he was supposed to be doing, then…' he winced '…died, it made me curious.' He gave a smile and held up his hand. 'And then I reached the luxury resort, and within a day…' he pulled a face '…truth is, I was bored. Even if I hadn't met Harry on the plane I would still have come looking for something else to do. A way to volunteer or help.'

'What's the deal with being a prince? Why keep it a secret?'

He wanted to throw his hands up in frustration. No one really understood what it was like. The constant scrutiny. Living your life under the spotlight. Saying hello to a woman and having a story in the press the next day saying that you were getting married.

He gave a slow nod of his head. 'When I'm in Corinez, I'm Prince Philippe, through and through. It's my role. I've been brought up to fulfil that purpose. But I had a few years' leeway—time to come and train as a doctor and gain experience that would help me fulfil my ultimate duty when it was time to go home.'

'And is it time to go home now?'

He closed his eyes for a second. 'It is.' He took a deep breath. 'Come with me.'

The more he thought about things, the more it all made sense in his head. 'Come with me and help me set up a safe haven scheme in Corinez. The last patient I dealt with back home was a baby who'd been abandoned. We don't have a national healthcare system. People have to pay for all medical services, and finances have changed in Corinez. The recession has hit hard. We have more and more incidents of babies being abandoned. I hope to campaign for free maternal healthcare in Corinez—at least to start with. But I also need to put in place a scheme like you have. I need to ensure these babies can be safe, can be looked after.' He leaned forward and grasped her hands. 'And you can help me do that.'

She pulled herself back. 'But…' Nothing else followed. She seemed stuck for words.

'Think of it as a mix between a holiday and a humanitarian effort. I can show you a little of Corinez and you can advise me on the best way to set up the scheme while you get your visa sorted out and look for another job that you really want.'

She was still stunned. He kept going, conscious he was babbling, but he just wanted her to agree. He didn't want to leave here without her. She looked up at him. 'Look at the trouble I've just had with London. Won't I need a visa to work in Corinez—no matter what role I'm doing?'

He waved his hand. 'That's one of the few perks of being a prince. I can sort that for you.' His gaze connected with hers. 'You've already told me that you've got the time here covered. There's no need for you to stay. You could look for some kind of temporary cover or sick-leave type of job—but do you really want that? Why not try something different? Come with me, help me in Corinez. Help me set up the same scheme you have here.'

He hadn't moved his hands. They were still clasped over hers.

'You're a prince,' she said again, looking him square in the eye.

He nodded again and gave her a resigned smile. 'Yes, I'm a prince.'

She wrinkled her nose. 'Where, exactly, is Corinez again?'

'It's near France, Italy and Monaco.'

She blinked. 'What?'

He shook his head. 'Forget it, it's not that important. It's an island. It has mountains that people ski on, it has a casino—no, scratch that, it has *many* casinos—it has a huge port. We laugh and call it the cruise ship depot because so many stop there.'

Arissa let out a long slow breath. 'You're a prince.'

He smiled. 'Yeah, you said that, a few times. I am a prince. It's not gonna change. But what *can* change is what you can help me do. Come with me, Arissa. Come with me to Corinez. Be my champion.'

'Your champion?'

He smiled. 'It's what I always say to my patients when they have to take a deep breath for something.'

It was as if something flicked in her brain. She smiled then spoke carefully. 'This project. I won't be in the spotlight. I won't have to deal with press. I won't have to be…anything?'

She shook her head. His heart gave a lurch. She was considering coming. She was actually considering coming.

He didn't know exactly what was behind this, but it wasn't the first time she'd told him she didn't want to be in the spotlight. And right now he would agree to anything.

'Arissa, if you agree to come we can focus entirely on the project. You won't need to worry about anything else.'

He could see her holding her breath, and he held his too, waiting for her answer.

'No publicity,' she reiterated.

'No publicity,' he agreed.

She licked her lips and waited a few moments before she replied. 'Okay, then, Prince Philippe, show me your country.'

CHAPTER EIGHT

SHE COULDN'T HELP but stare out of the window of the plane, still not really believing that she was actually doing this.

Beneath her, Corinez was revealed through smoky clouds. The high mountains, busy harbour and rich city stretched out under her gaze. Philippe was preoccupied, talking to the man who'd appeared and been introduced as Philippe's personal secretary.

All of this was becoming scarily real.

She felt the undercarriage on the plane go down and they glided to a halt on a long runway. There was no Customs. No queues.

Instead they exited the plane straight into a white stretch limousine.

As soon as they stepped onto the tarmac she sensed a change in Philippe. He wasn't just the nonchalant doctor who offered to help out when required.

Now, he was Prince Philippe, and even though

he tried to be self-effacing it was apparent the people around him wouldn't allow him to be anything other than their Prince.

He was at ease amongst them. He disappeared for a few moments and the secretary bent to murmur in her ear. 'He has to have a quick chat with our local press, don't worry. He'll only be a few minutes. His Highness is good at giving them exactly what they want, in the minimum time possible.'

He had a strange kind of grin on his face as he said those words and she wasn't quite sure what he meant. The thought of dealing with the press sent uneasy prickles down her spine. But five minutes later Philippe appeared again and they were whisked off in the white limousine.

'I am supposed to call you Your Highness now?' she asked as she sank back into the soft leather upholstery.

He shook his head. 'You call me Philippe—or whatever name you think suits me at the time.'

She gave a half-frown. 'I'm not sure how that will go down with the rest of the people around you.'

He waved his hand. 'Don't worry about them. You're my guest—they know that. If there's anything you need, or want, you just have to say the word.'

She wasn't quite sure how she felt about that either. Arissa had spent her life doing things for herself and sorting herself out. Asking someone else for something wasn't really in her mindset and she wasn't sure it could be.

'When do we start work?' she asked, moving on to a subject she felt more comfortable with.

'As soon as we're settled.' The limousine started climbing a road winding up one of the nearby mountains. He gave her a knowing smile. 'The jet lag usually hits tomorrow, so we'll start the day after that.'

'I'd like to start as soon as we can.'

He kept smiling. 'What can I say?' He nodded his head at her. 'Your wish is my command.'

She watched as the hilly green countryside rapidly started to turn white. 'You have snow at this time of year?'

He leaned over next to her, letting her catch a whiff of his aftershave. 'We have snow all year round if you're high enough up the mountain. It's one of the few places where you can ski all year round. Down in the city can be in the middle of a heatwave, but up in the mountains the snow will still be lying.'

She gave a shiver. 'I'm not entirely sure I've brought the right wardrobe. Summer and winter in the same day?'

His eyes were gleaming. 'Welcome to Corinez.'

She settled back in the seat as the limousine turned through a set of ornate gates and up to a large grey and white stone four-storey palace, complete with turrets.

'You actually live in a palace?' she asked as her eyes tried to take in the view.

He wiggled his hand. 'There's some debate about that. We call it a palace, but apparently it's the same design as some Edwardian castle back in England. Worldwide travel wasn't common then. I think the designer might have thought that no one would realise he'd used the same plans twice.'

Arissa pressed her face closer to the car window. 'It looks beautiful.'

He gave a nod. 'It is. But the gardens are actually my favourite part. There's a fountain, a maze and extensive oriental gardens.'

The car slowly stopped and the chauffeur got out to open the door. Arissa walked up the impressive front steps, her heart tripping a little in her chest. Yip. She was right back in that childhood fantasy. She'd never imagined that she'd actually meet a prince for real—it still hadn't sunk in.

The inside of the castle was just as impressive as the outside. Arissa was led up one side of a curved dual staircase and along an impressive corridor to a suite.

Even though the style was Georgian, parts of the castle were decidedly updated. Arissa's room was decorated in shades of green and gold. The bed was at least six feet across, with sumptuous bedding. The carpet was so thick her feet sank into it and she wiggled her toes in pleasure. The bathroom was bigger than her bedroom back home, as was her dressing room. She gave a little laugh as the palace aide placed her single suitcase in the middle of the dressing room. It looked so lonely there—her clothing wouldn't take up even a tenth of the space in this room.

She smiled as she wandered through the suite, shaking her head at the expanse of it. Someone had run a bath for her already, with lavender scents drifting towards her and purple petals floating on the bathwater. The main windows in the suite looked out over the stunning gardens and even from here she could see the light dusting of snow across them.

She took a breath and sat down on the window ledge. She was here. In Corinez. What on earth was she thinking about?

There were some chocolates on the table in front of her, along with a bottle of wine chilling in a cooler and two glasses. Who had done this?

Was it Philippe? Did he mean to come along and join her, or was this standard for any guest?

She just wasn't sure. She moved from the window ledge and sat down in one of the surprisingly comfortable chairs that looked out over the gardens. It was more beautiful than she could ever have imagined. Every little girl's fantasy.

But, for all its beauty and grandeur, somewhere out there—just like at home in Temur Sapora—could be a young girl or woman, contemplating giving up her baby.

A baby like her.

With the light dusting of snow at the very back of the gardens she could understand that where a baby was left could be the difference between life and death.

She had a reason to be here. She had a function. Philippe knew she was committed to the programme—even though he didn't really know her reasons. Those were hers to keep.

She glanced over at the sumptuous bed and breathed in the lavender scent coming from the bathroom, and while for tonight she might enjoy the lifestyle, she wouldn't forget the people she was here to help.

How could she? Arissa was a doctor. And she

was an abandoned baby. And no matter the love she'd experienced in her life—that was what she would always be.

CHAPTER NINE

PHILIPPE KNOCKED ON the door hesitantly, wondering if Arissa had managed to shake off the jet lag.

She opened the door, bright and breezy, wearing jeans and a red shirt. 'Ready to start work?' she asked.

He laughed. 'I wasn't sure you'd be ready.'

She held out her hands. 'I'm ready to see breakfast Corinez-style, and I definitely want to see where you intend to place the safe haven cots.'

He gave a firm nod as his stomach gave a little flip. Even not seeing her last night had been hard. She hadn't answered when he'd knocked on the door, and when he'd dared to peek inside she'd been sleeping soundly beneath the canopy of the large bed.

It had been so tempting to take a step inside—but Philippe would never do a thing like that. He was just happy that his guest was comfortable.

The morning sun gleamed behind her from the large windows, almost creating a halo above her dark curls. He could see every curve in her jeans and fitted shirt. She really had no idea just how gorgeous she was. He loved the fact she was ready to start. He loved her enthusiasm. But more than anything he loved the fact she'd agreed to come to his country with him. Part of him couldn't help but hope she might love it even a little as much as he did. He held out his elbow towards her, inviting her to slip her arm in his. 'Your wish is my command.'

And he meant it.

The journey down into the city was short. He took one of the cars from the palace gardens and waved away their chauffeur and security staff.

He could have gone to one of the many exclusive restaurants, but instead he took her to a well-established commercial coffee shop with chains around the world. Arissa clearly felt at home there as she could rhyme off her order by heart. It seemed that the menu didn't change the world over. The barista only raised one eyebrow when she clearly recognised Philippe, but the merest shake of his head was enough for her to realise not to say anything.

They settled at a table in the corner with their coffee and croissants as Philippe explained some of their surroundings. 'We're in the east side of the city. This has always been the poorer side of the city, but in the last few years things have taken a downward turn. Unemployment has risen and because Corinez doesn't have an adequate social security system in place, or free healthcare, the few cases of abandoned babies has increased in the last year.'

She met his gaze thoughtfully. 'You could have your work cut out for you.'

'That's why you're here.'

'Have you considered someplace that would be central enough for a safe haven cot?'

He nodded. 'I think we're going to go along the same route as yourself and use the fire stations. Our hospital would have been our first option, but, like your clinic, the road to the hospital is too well used, too open. I'm not sure that someone would feel confident to leave their baby at the hospital without fear of being discovered. The whole ethos behind the safe haven is that a woman can leave her child safely and without exposure to herself—no matter how much we'd really like to know who she is, and if she's safe too. Our fire station is in a central area, but not quite as busy—not quite as exposed—and there are always staff based in the station, so the baby wouldn't be left for any long period of time. It makes more sense to arrange for the safe haven to be placed there.'

She nodded. 'Do you have notes about where any of the other abandoned babies have been left in Corinez?'

He nodded. 'I've spoken to my police colleagues. There have been four in the last year. One left near the hospital, but not quite at the main entrance. Another left in a shop doorway in the east end of the city. A third near the fire station, and a fourth in the car park at the back of a local supermarket in the dead of night.'

His heart squeezed; he was worried she might ask the next question he just didn't want to answer. But her brain headed in another direction.

Arissa gulped. 'Have you ever managed to find any of the mothers?'

'Only one. She was admitted to hospital after collapsing in the street. She had a severe infection caused by the birth.'

He could see the next question in her eyes. 'She didn't want to be reunited with her baby. She had some other serious health conditions. The pregnancy had caused enormous strain on her body, and because she had no healthcare…'

He held up his hands and she finished the sentence for him. 'She just couldn't manage.'

He nodded. It was almost as if she could see the pressure he felt hanging above him.

Her fingers brushed against his and he couldn't help it, his fingers twitched and started to intertwine with hers. It seemed natural. It seemed honest. 'What are you going to do about the healthcare system in Corinez?' she asked.

The million-dollar question—or the more than million-euro question as it would turn out to be. He sighed deeply and gave a slow shake of his head. 'It needs to be overhauled. It doesn't meet the needs of our people.' He gave a wry smile. 'Unless, of course, you're a billionaire. We have dozens of private clinics and hospitals. Corinez is like a plastic surgeon's dream—because we have the climate and the geography, lots of people come here to have surgery and recuperate. But because so many investors like to make money from the private hospitals and clinics, it means our national hospital and community clinics are short-changed, in staffing levels and finance.'

'You can't staff your hospitals?'

He leaned his head on one hand. 'Nurses in the private hospitals get paid at a much higher rate than the state hospital. It's hard to keep staff.'

'And you don't have the budget to pay them more?'

He nodded. 'Exactly.'

She leaned back in her chair and looked around. 'You have a lifetime of work here, Philippe.'

He nodded. 'I know I do. I just need to start having courageous conversations with some of our parliament members and some of our investors. I know where I need to start. It has to be maternity care. If I can even persuade them to make that part of the healthcare system free, then we can try to ensure the best start for every child.'

He waited a few moments, conscious that they were now starting to get a few glances from people from the surrounding tables who seemed to be focusing on their intertwined hands.

He stood up quickly. Arissa looked surprised. 'Come on,' he said. 'Let's go and have a look at the fire station, and then I have somewhere I want to take you.'

She looked a little surprised by his sudden move and after a few seconds took his outstretched hand. 'Okay, then, Philippe, like I said before, show me Corinez.'

* * *

She loved it. She loved this place already. It was clear that people here respected their Prince—even if they did seem a little obsessed by him.

Everywhere they went there were nudges and side glances. She tried to stay focused. To look at the geography and the people around them. Poverty wasn't evident at the first glance, but dig a little beneath the surface—go to the right places—and it was there to see.

They visited a few community centres and spoke to some of the clientele. She met the chief of the fire and rescue service and was bowled over by his enthusiasm for the project. He immediately agreed to call his equivalent in Temur Sapora.

She liked the fact they were more or less travelling incognito. Philippe handled the busy streets easily and by the time dusk started to fall she couldn't hide the yawn.

'Tired?' he asked as they drove back towards the palace.

She gave a nod. 'I feel as if I need forty winks. But if I do that, I'll probably be up half the night.'

He gave a shrug. 'It doesn't matter. Do it. And if you want company in the middle of the night you know where I am.'

She wasn't quite sure how he meant that to

come out, but tingles were already dancing along her skin.

'I don't need you again until tomorrow afternoon. We're going to visit the state hospital to see if you can give me some ideas of where to start with the overhaul.'

She stifled another yawn and tried not to let her head nod. She couldn't quite believe how exhausted she felt. 'How did I ever get through being a junior doctor?' She shook her head. 'Sometimes we were awake for nearly forty hours.'

'But you weren't crossing two time zones,' he replied. 'Believe me, it makes a difference.'

'I guess it does,' she said as they pulled up to the palace garages. She gave a frown. 'I'm not quite sure how to get to my room from here.'

He parked the car and walked around, opening her door for her. 'Don't worry, I'll show you.'

There was an elevator to take them upstairs. As soon as the doors slid closed Philippe turned to face her. He seemed so far away.

'What do you think of Corinez so far?' She could hear the edge of uncertainty in his voice.

She took a step closer and put her hand on his arm. From here she could smell his aftershave, see the shadow starting to show along his jawline. 'I like it,' she replied honestly. 'And I want to find out more.' She licked her lips and moved even closer. 'And I like it even more that I can see how passionate you are about your country, and how much you want to make things better.'

He looked down at her, his hand sliding behind her waist. 'That's exactly how you are about Temur Sapora.' He lowered his head so his lips were only inches from hers. His breath warmed her skin. 'Maybe it makes us a good match.'

'Maybe it does,' she agreed as she moved closer until her lips were only millimetres from his. She couldn't help but smile.

'I sense you might be trouble,' he teased.

'I think you might be right.' She smiled as his lips met hers. Every cell in her body started reacting. It had been too long—even though it was only a few days. She moved her hand up to behind his head, letting her fingers run through his thick dark hair. He tasted of coffee, strawberries and apples—all the things they'd eaten today—but it was his smell that enticed her more. She couldn't place it, too many pheromones—or maybe that was exactly what it was, maybe they were more of a match than he thought and his pheromones were hooking her in. She didn't care. All she cared about was this moment. Her body melded to his. She was already tired and somehow leaning against him made her instincts soar.

She didn't even notice when the elevator doors slid open.

What she did notice was someone clearing their throat. Loudly.

They sprang apart and Philippe stiffened. 'Luka.' He nodded to the dark-suited man at the door. 'You're looking for me?'

The man started talking in a low voice, his eyes darting over to Arissa and giving her the most dismissive of glances. She was instantly uncomfortable. She waited a few seconds then slid out of the elevator before the doors closed again and started walking down the corridor, praying she was heading in the right direction.

Her heart was thrumming against her chest, part from the reaction to Philippe and part from the adrenaline coursing through her body in annoyance.

She turned a corner and sighed in relief as she recognised the corridor, finding her room quickly and closing the door behind her. She took off her jacket and shoes and flung herself down on the bed. Her head was spinning.

Last time she'd kissed him he was just Philippe, the doctor who was helping at the clinic. This time she'd kissed Prince Philippe of Corinez. Did it feel different? Her heart told her no, but her brain couldn't quite decide.

And as she closed her eyes, she still wasn't quite sure.

There was a thud. She twitched. A few seconds later there was another. This time she was more awake. She blinked and sat up in bed. What was that?

She'd fallen asleep fully clothed. The room was almost dark, the only light filtering in from outside. She shook her head and stood up. What time was it?

There was yet another thud. This time she located the sound and watched as snow slid down the window.

Really?

She looked out of the window and almost laughed when she realised what had been green grass earlier was now completely covered with snow. It wasn't particularly heavy, so whoever was throwing snowballs must be taking their time to scrounge up enough snow.

She shook her head and opened the old-fashioned window, listening to it creak and hoping it wasn't going to land on the hard slabs below. Five minutes in a palace and she might wreck the place.

Another snowball sailed directly past her

ear, this one landing on the carpet in the room. 'Hey!' she shouted, turning around to try and pick up the snow. She scattered the snow back out of the window and leaned out, trying to catch a glimpse of who was outside. Turned out she was looking too far away.

Philippe was directly under her window, dressed in a navy-blue jacket. He had a mischievous look on his face.

'Hey, sleepyhead. Want to go for a walk?'

She leaned her elbows on the window ledge. 'I thought you said I was trouble,' she teased.

'Maybe I like trouble.' He was grinning up at her. He held out his hands and spun around. 'Let me show you the gardens while they're dusted with snow. It never usually comes this far down the mountain this time of year. By morning, I guarantee it will all be gone.'

She shook her head. 'Snow, in the middle of summer. It's definitely weird.'

'Come on.' He waved her down. 'Grab a jacket and some boots and let's go.'

It only took a few moments to get ready. She threw on a whole new set of clothes: new jeans, a green top, a pair of boots and the only thicker jacket she'd brought with her. She laughed as she zipped it. It was navy blue. They'd look like a matching pair.

She made her way down the stairs and out

into the cold night air. Philippe had moved nearer the door and was standing waiting for her. 'What time is it?' she asked. She hadn't even had a chance to look at the clock. It felt as if she'd slept for ever. She wrinkled her nose. 'Did I miss dinner?' she asked as she stared up at the black night sky.

He laughed. 'You definitely missed dinner. It's nearly midnight.'

'Is it?' She felt her eyes widen. 'I can't believe I slept so long.'

He leaned over and touched her nose with one cold finger. 'Jet lag. Told you.'

She gave a little yelp and jumped back. 'Hey, you're freezing.'

He reached out and grabbed her hand. 'And I plan on getting you cold too. It's summer. Who can wear gloves in the middle of summer?'

She shivered as his cold hand closed around hers. But she didn't pull away. She didn't want to. 'You obviously should,' she quipped. 'But, hey, I can make the ultimate sacrifice and try and heat you up.'

'I like the sound of that.'

He pulled her closer and put his arm around her shoulders. Even though the air was chilly she was much more conscious of the length of his body next to hers and the heat coming from it.

She shook her head as they started walking across the gardens. 'Can't believe I completely slept through dinner.'

He grinned and shrugged. 'I could have left you to sleep, but I think you'd probably have woken up about three or four in the morning and not be able to get back to sleep. This way, you're up for a few hours and will hopefully get back to sleep before breakfast rolls around.'

'Where are we going for breakfast tomorrow, then?' she asked.

He gave her a sideways glance. 'I thought you might like to sleep a little later.'

'And miss out on breakfast with you?' Her stomach gave a squeeze. Maybe he was trying to let her down gently, or maybe he was just too busy to spend time with her. After all, what did a prince do all day—particularly one who wanted to reform his health service? The reality was he probably didn't have time for her at all.

He started to talk but she shook her head. 'Forget it. You're busy. I get it. I'll just see you at the hospital in the afternoon like we planned.'

They were walking behind a high hedge and turned a corner and she let out a little gasp. 'Wow.'

The gardens were split level. 'Left or right?' he asked.

Beneath them on one side looked like the oriental gardens, even in the dark night she could see the outline of a pagoda, an arched bridge and hear the sounds of waterfalls. On the other side was a large maze. In the dark it looked quite ominous.

'Let's go to the right,' she said. 'Show me around the oriental gardens.'

'Chicken,' he teased as he led her down the steps towards the gardens.

She shook her head. 'Not at all. I just think the oriental gardens look interesting.'

There was only one old-fashioned lamp post at the entrance to the oriental gardens casting a dim light on the path before them. He walked her slowly around the large gardens. Under the stars she could see the pagoda was painted red and gold with intricate styling. The light dusting of snow made it look even more magical.

Philippe showed her the Kwanzan cherry trees, the bamboo, flowering plums and Japanese black pine. He led her across one of the bridges and stopped in the middle, looking down into the dark pond beneath them. 'I'm not sure if you can see but the pond is full of koi—they're known as the fish of emperors.

Arissa bent forward for a better look. 'If there's snow falling, isn't it too cold for them?'

she asked. The water rippled as she caught a flick of an orange tail just beneath them.

He nodded. 'When it's cold they tend to gather just under the bridge where it gives more shelter. But we never usually have any problems with them. They're hardy little creatures.'

He moved his arm from her shoulders and took her by the hand, leading her around the pond edges, pointing out the weeping willow trees and water lilies. Eventually the path led them back to the entrance.

He nodded ahead. 'Okay, have you managed to work up enough courage yet for the maze?'

She put one hand on her hip. 'I've got the feeling you'll have a distinct advantage here. You've grown up with this maze. You could probably go through it blindfolded.'

He opened his mouth in teasing horror. 'Were you spying on me when I was a kid?'

'Hardly.' She pressed her lips together for a second. She had to say something. She wasn't sure when else she would get the opportunity. 'I didn't know anything about you, Philippe, because I didn't generally read about princes when I was a kid.'

The air was still around them. He looked down for a second. It was clear he knew where this would be heading. 'Arissa...' he started, letting his voice trail off.

She stepped forward and gave a little shake of her head, pressing her hand to his chest. She wasn't afraid to touch him. She wasn't afraid of familiarity. But she had to let him know how she felt.

'You worked with me for nearly two weeks, Philippe. You never said a word. I felt foolish when you finally told me you were a prince.'

He sighed and nodded his head, waiting a few seconds before lifting his gaze to meet hers. 'I didn't want to ruin anything.'

'With the truth?'

It was obvious he was frustrated. 'I wasn't there to be a prince. I wasn't even there to be a doctor. I went to Temur Sapora for a rest—but you know how that turned out.' He held out his hands. 'I had two weeks of unplanned nothingness. Two weeks to get my head around what had happened here, and the role I was coming back to. Changes have been needed for years, and, although I've always known that, I've never really known where to start. The last few months have made me realise it has to be maternity services. It goes hand in hand with the safe haven work.' He stopped and reached up and ran his hands through her curls. 'And then, there was you.'

He gave her a smile that warmed her all the way to her toes.

'Me?' All of a sudden it was difficult to swallow.

'You. Arissa Cotter. Mrs No Nonsense. Mrs Plans. The woman with a fantastic career path at her feet, but still having a commitment to, and love for the place you came from.'

The edges of her lips turned upwards. 'Isn't that normal?'

He moved his hand to her shoulder. 'Maybe. It's normal for you. And it's normal for me. But for lots of other people…' He shook his head. 'Lots of other people just seem to want to leave their past and home behind them. Like ancient history.'

She took a few seconds to answer. 'But I love my home.'

'And that's part of what I love about you.'

She froze. She knew it was just a figure of speech but she couldn't help but instantly be a little scared. Love was a big word to say around someone.

Philippe didn't seem to notice her tensing. He just kept talking, his hand drifting back to tangle in her hair. 'But it wasn't just that. You seemed to like spending time with me, *just* being me. Not a prince. Not someone who could help change in their country. And I liked that.' He stopped for a second, his gaze locking with hers. 'Because the truth is, for me, that's different. The last few months working in Corinez? People treat me like I'm some kind of special event—not a real doctor. But working with you in Temur Sapora? I loved the anonymity. I loved the fact I was just Philippe. Nothing else. Because here, in Corinez, I never get to just be Philippe. They want Prince Philippe. They don't want me.' He put his hand to his chest again. 'All my life that's who I've been, that's who I'll always be. I've never had the chance to just be Philippe. Coming to Temur Sapora was the first time in thirty years I've had that opportunity.'

He let out a wry laugh. 'And maybe I've got this all wrong, but I think you quite liked Philippe.'

She stood very still for a minute, letting her breath steam in the air between them. She was trying hard to understand what kind of life he'd led. The pressure put on him. Things she'd never once in a lifetime thought about—never had reason to.

She reached up and touched his face. 'You're different here. I noticed it from the second you stepped off the plane. Here, you're Prince Philippe. I thought I already knew you, but I guess I only know part of you.'

He shook his head. 'That's not true. The person at the clinic, the person who tried to cook you dinner, the person who swam in the ocean with you. That's me. That's who I am. You know the real Philippe.'

She shook her head and gave a sad kind of smile. Her heart felt a little heavy. 'For me to get to know you, I need to know all of you—not just the person you want me to see.'

She could sense he was getting anxious. He thudded his hand against his heart. 'This is the real me. You know me. You met me back on Temur Sapora.'

But she shook her head again. 'I met part of you. Not all of you.' She held out her hands. 'This is the place where you feel most at home. This is where you lived your life and grew up. I know and liked Philippe Aronaz. I've still to make my mind up about Prince Philippe of Corinez.'

She tipped her head to one side. 'You might not know this, but you have a bit of a reputation as being a playboy. Or being on—' she put her fingers in the air '—"the most eligible royals in the world" list.'

He visibly cringed. 'I hate all that stuff.'

'There's a world of pictures out there, Philippe, of you with a gorgeous girl wearing million-dollar jewellery and clothes on your arm. *Lots* of girls.'

He leaned forward and caught her face with

his hands. 'But you are more beautiful than all of them.'

She shook her head. 'But that's not me. That won't ever be me. I want to keep doing the job that I love and keep my head down. I don't want to be photographed. I don't want my life picked apart by nosey reporters. I don't want to be one of "those" people who court the media. I'm not sure that part of your life will ever change. And I wouldn't ask you to change your life for me. This, this is your destiny.'

There was silence for a few seconds, because both of them knew that was true.

He spoke slowly, his words almost pleading. 'But you're here, now. You came halfway around the world with me. For a guy you met in a clinic two weeks ago. That must mean something. Don't give up on something before it's even started. You came here to help me work. Let's do it. Help me. Be a part of the changes I want to make here.'

She could see the enthusiasm emanating from every part of him and it made her ache. From the second she'd looked down from her window tonight, a little part of her had worried.

Things were different here, and, even though she'd expected them to be, it was only now starting to sink in.

She couldn't ever get back the guy she'd

kissed and swum in the ocean with. No matter how much she wanted him.

She had no job to go to right now. It made sense to stay here. But the more time she spent in Philippe's company the more she realised she was gradually losing a little part of her heart to him—a guy she could never really be with.

Did she really want to do that?

She licked her lips. 'I'll stay, just for a while. But I'll be applying for other jobs. I need to find another paediatric oncology centre where there is a suitable position—and this time, I'll sort out my own visa.'

There was a flash of disappointment in his eyes and she hated that she'd put it there. But honesty was better.

If she'd known he was a prince would she have let him close to her? Probably not, and that made her stomach twist in a way she didn't like at all. Because this man standing in front of her was the man who'd made electricity flow through her skin. The man who'd kissed her in a way that no one else ever had. She couldn't ignore that. No matter how much other stuff was going on in her head.

She looked around. It was pitch black. They were in the middle of the palace gardens in the dead of night. For a few minutes more she could try to forget about the prince part. She could try and remember the gorgeous man she'd wrapped her legs around in the ocean and raced to the buoy.

She stepped forward and gave him a smile. 'How about, for now, we just be you, and me?'

She saw his shoulders relax. It was as if a weight had just lifted from him. 'Show me your maze, Philippe,' she said quietly, leaving all the titles to the side.

He slid his hand into hers in agreement. 'Come on, then.'

They entered the maze. The hedges were at least eight feet tall; there was no way either of them could see over. 'I should have tried to memorise what this looked like when we were on the steps above,' she murmured.

He gave a laugh. 'Lots of people try to do that. Most of the time it doesn't work.' He turned around so he was walking backwards and facing her.

She wrinkled her nose. 'Isn't there a thing you're supposed to do in mazes?' She held up her hand. 'That's it, if you keep your left hand running along the hedges you'll always find the way out.'

He shook his head. 'Old wives' tale. No truth in it at all.'

'Really?' She was suspicious now, not sure whether to believe him or not. The further they went into the maze, the darker it got. Shadows seemed to lurk around every corner. 'I think I might have preferred this in the daytime,' she joked.

'Oh, come on,' he teased. 'What do you think is in here? Lions, tigers and bears?'

She shook her head at the film reference. 'I was thinking more like goblins, warlocks and trolls.'

'Ouch,' he said. 'What kind of kids' stories did you read?'

'The good ones.'

They kept walking. He backwards and she forwards. It was odd. It was cute. They were shielded from the world. She liked it that way. Here they could be anyone they wanted to be. Here, she could be with anyone she wanted to be.

They turned a corner and the maze changed. There was a paved area with a star in the middle and a wrought-iron bench. 'Is this it? Have we reached the centre?'

He nodded and pulled her down onto the bench. She perched on the edge of his lap. 'So,' she said with a smile on her face. 'Now we've reached the middle, what happens next?'

The words hung in the air between them. They both knew exactly what she meant.

Philippe slid his hands up around her neck.

'How about you make good on the sacrifice you offered to make a little earlier?'

She frowned. 'What one was that?'

He pulled her closer. 'The one where you offered to heat me up,' he whispered, his lips making a trail down the side of her face.

Their skin brushed together. Full of intent. 'Oh, I have a rule,' she said huskily, 'that I always make good on my promises.'

A smile danced across her lips. 'Somehow I like that,' he said as his lips met hers.

And for a few moments she forgot about everything else. About the palace. About the press. And the fact she was kissing a prince. And just concentrated on the man whose lips were setting her world on fire.

CHAPTER TEN

By the time afternoon came around she was anxious to get started. The jet lag finally seemed to have eked its way out of her system, and her brain could only focus on how much time she'd spent kissing Philippe last night.

Her brain told her everything about it was wrong. Silly. Nothing could ever come of it. They were almost at opposite ends of a scale.

But her heart? It seemed to defy every piece of logic her brain could throw at her.

She took a quick glance in the mirror and pulled her fitted black suit jacket straight. They were visiting the hospital today so she could give him some feedback and advice about his future plans. She'd decided on the more professional look. She wanted people to take her seriously, to know that she was always committed to providing good health services. She picked up her bag and gave her lips a swipe with rose-coloured lipstick. The knee-length skirt and fitted jacket were smart—she knew that. But her bright blue shirt gave the splash of colour that revealed a bit more of the person that she was. Most professionals would pair the suit with heels but Arissa had spent enough hours in hospitals to know better and she slid on a pair of comfortable flats.

The knock at the door was almost simultaneous with her pulling it open. 'Oh,' she said in surprise.

Philippe was standing in a dark blue suit, paired with pale blue shirt and dark tie. She hadn't seen him since last night and that first sight took her breath away.

He gave a casual grin. 'You're ready. Perfect. Do you need to eat before we go?'

She shook her head. 'Nope. All ready. Let's go. I can't wait to see the hospital.'

He pulled a face. 'There's so much work to be done there. Don't set your expectations too high. I keep telling myself if I want to build a proper health service for the country, I have to start somewhere.' He gestured his elbow towards her and she slid her arm into his.

'Well, that's why I'm here. I've worked in Malaysia, the US, did a spell as a student in England, and have volunteered for Doctors Without Borders in Romania. You've travelled too, you'll have seen enough health service systems to know what you want for Corinez.'

He gave a nod and led her along the corridor. Neither of them mentioned the kiss. Neither of them mentioned the conversation last night.

And to be honest, she was glad.

He knew he was only scratching the surface of the problem. Both in the hospital, and with Arissa.

He'd spent most of last night wondering what he'd done. He'd invited her here because he'd really, really wanted her to come. He couldn't deny the attraction between them. He couldn't pretend that it didn't matter that he knew Arissa liked him for just being him. It meant more than she could ever know.

But some of the things she'd said last night had thrown him sideways. He wasn't *him*. He would never just be *him*. He would always be Prince Philippe—no matter how much he tried to hide from it.

As a child he'd thought it was normal to be photographed and in the media constantly. It hadn't bothered him—more than a few of his teenage misdemeanours had been captured for the world to see. The Playboy Prince tag had been following him around for the last few years as well.

But now, as an adult, when his time of freedom was gone—when his time to return and help shape the healthcare changes had arrived—it was making him more than a little uncomfortable.

For a guy who'd always known who he was and exactly what his role would be, he found himself questioning *everything.*

And that bothered him more than he could ever say out loud. It wasn't even a conversation he could have with anyone else.

But as he showed Arissa around the hospital he got more and more uncomfortable.

She shone. That was the only way he could describe her. She got down on her knees to talk to the kids in the children's unit. She made several suggestions about gaps in services. Both for children and for babies and mothers. She was good at linking pieces of the puzzle together—throwing in things he hadn't yet considered. She challenged him. She made him think.

She talked through the most basic maternity care. Then, they talked about the maternity care he would really like to offer. She helped him make realistic targets and goals. And he needed that. He needed someone to keep him grounded and make the plans in his head into something more tangible.

But they didn't spend all their time in maternity services. Arissa wanted to see around the whole hospital.

She sat for a long time, holding the hand of a war veteran who wanted to reminisce with someone.

The staff and patients loved her. She was relaxed. She knew when to laugh, and when to be serious. He'd always known she would do well here, but seeing how much Arissa got to be herself made him realise how much of a prince-like status he had to keep in place.

Even when they entered the emergency department he couldn't be himself. He walked around, pointing to equipment, suggesting upgrades, suggesting rearranging the trauma room. Several of the members of staff shot him strange looks. Uncomfortable looks. No one questioned him about making suggestions. They all just nodded meekly.

For a few minutes he wished he were back in the clinic in Temur Sapora.

Somewhere he was no longer a prince.

It was different here. Even walking through a department seemed to cause an 'atmosphere'. Something Philippe was becoming more and more aware of.

'What's wrong?' Arissa was in front of him,

her wide brown eyes showing a hint of concern. 'Are you okay?'

He gave himself a shake, trying to smooth out the edges he knew he was exposing. 'I'm fine. Just…there's a lot to think about. A lot I'll need to change.'

She nodded. 'This is a huge job, Philippe.' She gave him a soft smile. 'But remember, you've got a lifetime to change all this. Start small. Start manageable.'

He ran his hands through his hair. 'Like we talked about?'

She nodded. 'You know you want to start with maternity services. Look at your minimum care standards. Look at your population. How many births do you have? Think about numbers. How can you make this realistic? Recruit obstetricians. Recruit midwives. Recruit lab staff for the extra blood work, sonographers for the baby scans. It ties in with the implementation of the safe haven project.'

He knew it all made sense. But he couldn't help but say something else. He'd seen how much she'd thrived in this environment today. 'What about paediatrics? We don't have any specialists like you. We don't have anyone who specialises in paediatric haematology.' Enthusiasm was brimming over in him.

She tilted her head to the side. 'No. But you

can include something like that in plans for the future. Tackle maternity services. Then, in a few years, think about children's services.'

He lowered his voice. 'But if I started with paediatrics instead, I could offer you a job. I could get you to stay.'

She blinked. Shock written all over her face. It was clear he had blindsided her.

It was selfish. It was entirely selfish. It was ridiculous. But he couldn't shake the horrible dark cloud at the back of his head that kept whispering to him that soon she would be gone.

But Arissa stepped right up to him, looking him straight in the face with those big brown eyes. It was almost as if she could read his mind sometimes.

'Philippe,' she said quietly, with the hint of a smile on her lips. 'I love that you're thinking about me—in amongst the world of things you already have to do.'

She shook her head. 'But we both know how important it is that you get this right. You need to take a bit of time to consider everything. Probably write up a business plan. Discuss it with the other members of your committee and decide what is actually feasible.' She licked her lips and gave him a soft smile. 'And not let yourself be influenced by a girl who kissed you in a dark maze at night.'

Darn it. He wanted to kiss her again. She was right—and she was sensible enough to know that, even though he'd said the words out loud, it had only been a flash of an idea. Not anything tangible. At least not right now.

He hated that part.

She held up her hands. 'Maybe, in a few years—' she winked '—we can talk again. You could consider children's services in Corinez.'

She wasn't saying no. His heart gave a leap in his chest.

He slid his hand into hers as pieces in his brain slotted into place. She gave the briefest start of surprise, looking down at their joined hands. Maybe she hadn't expected him to show his affection in public. Before, they'd really been at arm's length while outside the palace. But he couldn't pretend that he wanted to be at arm's length from Arissa.

He could also see the way that everyone who'd come into contact with them had reacted to her.

After a few minutes in her company and listening to her intelligent conversation, the staff and directors of the hospital had looked at her with interest and respect. She seemed to be able to bring out the best in people. She knew how to engage. She knew how to act. And she knew how to listen—one of the biggest skills of a doctor.

Her manner was calm but enthusiastic. She was certainly at home within a hospital environment; it was almost like watching her bloom and grow. Whoever the hospital was in London that had let her slip through their fingers—they were clearly fools.

By the time they'd made their way back to the main entrance of the hospital the sky was beginning to grow dark and they'd stayed there more than three hours longer than originally had been planned.

Philippe gave a grateful smile to the staff that had accompanied them. Not one of them had complained. His own personal secretary had only made a few occasional glances at his watch and disappeared at one point to make a call to obviously reschedule something or another. It was as if everyone was as enthusiastic as he was. Most were full of some sort of ideas—even if they didn't really know where to start.

It seemed that most of the people who worked within the healthcare system in Corinez were ready for change. More than that—they were embracing it. If he could capture what was in the air right now and bottle it things might actually change. And Arissa was a big part of this.

She made him stop to consider ways to make it bite-sized and manageable. That was what he needed right now. It was as if she knew him better than he knew himself.

As they slid into the car that had pulled up outside for them he turned to face her.

But before he even had a chance to say a word she leaned across the car and put her head on his shoulder. ‘Oh, my goodness, I’m exhausted. It feels like being at the end of a twenty-four-hour shift.’ Her hand moved and rested against his chest. Her fingers gave a few anxious drums against his chest wall. ‘What do you think? Will you be able to make some plans?’

He stared down at the dark curls directly under his nose as the aroma from her orange shampoo drifted up around him. He couldn’t help but inhale. So much of today had been good. So much of the last couple of weeks had made his brain spin.

But the one thing that seemed entirely certain was the warmth and weight of the woman currently lying halfway across him. Their breaths were rising and falling in unison. He liked that. He liked that they seemed so in sync.

Last night it had seemed as if she was trying to take a step back. A step away from him and the life that he was designated to live. Now, he felt in perfect harmony.

'Oh, yes,' he said quietly. 'I hope to be able to make some plans.'

He breathed in slowly. 'Arissa?' He asked the question quietly, conscious that she already had her eyes half closed.

'Hmm?' She raised her head, her eyelids still mainly closed.

'There's something I'd like to ask you to do.'

This time her eyes opened a bit further. 'What?' she asked sleepily.

He smiled. 'There's something on at the palace in a few days. A ball—of sorts.'

She sat up with a confused expression on her face. 'But...'

He held up his hands. 'This isn't a normal royal ball. This one has no publicity, no press. It's just for my mother's oldest friends and family. We can go together and dance, and have fun. Nothing to worry about. You can...' he touched her cheek '...keep your head below the parapet.' He spoke carefully. 'Would you come with me, Arissa?'

She sat a little straighter. 'No press. No publicity. Only your mother's friends?'

He nodded. 'I have to admit my mother has a few friends. There will be a few other members of royal families across Europe.'

'But no press?' she asked again.

He smiled at her. 'No press. You get to have the fun of attending a ball with free-flowing champagne, a small orchestra, and a world of canapés.'

She wrinkled her nose and looked down at her black suit. 'I didn't exactly bring any kind of ball gown with me. In fact, I don't own any kind of ball gown.'

He gave a laugh. 'Well, in that case. I can either take you somewhere to shop and buy you something new, or you could talk to my sister, who has a wardrobe that covers three rooms—or, you can speak to my mother. She has a bit of a collection of ball gowns from throughout the years. Truth is, in other circumstances I think my mother would be known as a hoarder.'

Arissa blinked her tired eyes. 'How long do I have?'

He pulled a face. 'Less than two days,' he admitted.

She raised her eyebrows. 'What?' Now her eyes opened completely. 'Philippe Aronaz, you're giving me less than two days to find a ball gown for an event that will be filled with your family and friends?'

He shifted on the leather seat of the car. 'Yip. That would be about right.'

She nodded her head then gave him a sideways glance. 'Okay, so you're offering to take me to a ball where I can be on your arm, dance my heart out, and not worry about it being in the news?' She folded her hands in her lap. 'I haven't even met your mother yet—how can I ask to wear one of her old gowns?'

He shook his head. 'She's not been here. She's been in Austria. She'll be back tomorrow, and I can promise you right now that she'll be delighted if you wear one of her gowns. Every year she tries to persuade my sister to pick something from her collection.'

Arissa rested her head back on his shoulder. 'Okay, Philippe, you have a room full of dresses and you've invited me to a ball in the palace. It's like you jumped into my childhood and found one of my kids' fairy stories. How on earth could any girl say no to an invitation like that?'

He couldn't help but smile as a warm feeling spread through him. She'd said yes. It was the first time he'd ever taken someone to his mother's annual ball. He'd taken a variety of partners to various palace events throughout the years. Ones when he'd needed someone on his arm, at a time when he'd been expected to court the media. But he'd never taken anyone to his mother's private ball. This one was entirely different. He moved slightly, adjusting Arissa in his arms.

She smiled with her eyes still closed. 'Now, wake me up when we get back to the palace.'

The maid had shown her up to the room on the first floor of the palace. She gave a little gasp as she stepped into the large space. The walls were pale yellow and the large windows allowed light to stream into the room.

On one side of the room, away from the light of the windows, were row upon row of a multitude of dresses all shrouded in protective covers. The dresses were arranged like a rainbow with one range of colours flowing into the others.

Arissa's mouth fell open as she wandered along the rows, her hands reaching up to touch the odd dress to examine it a little closer.

The maid smiled. 'They're beautiful, aren't they?' She moved alongside Arissa. 'Is there a particular style you like best, or you find the most flattering? Or is there a colour you like best? I know all the dresses,' she said casually. 'I can probably point you in the right direction.'

It was like being the proverbial child in a sweet shop. Arissa's eyes were practically on stalks as she wandered along the rows. 'There's just so many,' she said in wonder. The maid shot her a smile and settled down in a chair in the corner of the room. There was a huge mirror on the wall close to her, along with a circular velvet curtain that swept around to give a private dressing area. This whole room was dedicated to the enjoyment of trying on these dresses. Every little girl's dream.

After a while she shook her head and held out her hands. 'The truth is, I have no idea where to start. I've never been to a ball—I don't know what's suitable and what's not.'

The maid came and stood in front of her, not hiding the fact that her discerning eye was sweeping up and down Arissa's frame.

'Will anything even fit me?' Arissa asked self-consciously.

The maid gave a smile. 'I think just about everything here will fit you. And if it doesn't? No problem. We have a seamstress on hand who can tweak any dress.' She put her hand to her mouth. 'Now...' she said. This time she started to walk around Arissa. 'What's your favourite part of yourself, and your least favourite part?'

Arissa tilted her head.

The maid smiled and continued. 'There's a whole bounty of dresses in here that I think will be perfect. But it's you that's wearing this dress, and you need to love it enough that you feel comfortable in it. There's no point in me making a suggestion of a dress with a low back if you feel self-conscious about showing skin.'

Arissa gave a nod. 'Okay, I understand. Nothing too revealing for me, then, please. And I'm a little on the short side.' She ran her hand across her stomach. 'And this is probably my worst bit, so nothing that clings too much and shows what I had for dinner.'

The maid laughed. She held out her hands to the array of rainbow dresses. 'You still haven't told me your favourite colour.'

Arissa looked down at the red shirt she was wearing today. 'I guess I like all colours. Preferably not black or white.'

The door opened and the maid turned in surprise. 'Your Majesty, forgive me. I wasn't aware you had returned.' She gestured towards Arissa. 'I was just helping Prince Philippe's guest select a dress for the ball.'

Arissa's feet had found themselves frozen to the floor. She watched as an elegant woman with her fine blonde hair swept up in a chignon came into the room. Her eyes met Arissa's and she gave her a wide smile.

'Ah-h, the doctor.' She walked towards Arissa with her arms outstretched. 'So you're the woman my son has been talking about so much.'

'I am?' She was stunned. She wasn't even

sure Philippe would have mentioned her at all to his mother.

'Maria Aronaz,' said the woman, clasping Arissa's hands in hers. Panic flooded through Arissa. Was she supposed to bow, curtsey? What did you do around royalty these days? How did you even address them?

Her brain focused on the maid's words. She dipped her head a little. 'It's a pleasure to meet you, Your Majesty. Thank you for welcoming me into your home.'

The woman kept her hands on Arissa's. Her eyes were warm but Arissa knew that the Queen was inspecting her to see if she was worthy of her son's attention. 'You are indeed beautiful,' the Queen said quietly as she squeezed Arissa's hands. 'And I hear that your home is as beautiful as ours.' She was watching Arissa carefully. 'Philippe has an enormous job ahead of him. Probably harder than the roles of his brother and sister.'

Arissa gave an uncomfortable gulp. The role of potential King would be hard enough, and being part of a finance committee wouldn't exactly be easy either. The Queen continued, 'Things are going to have to change in Corinez, and Philippe will have to weather the storm that comes alongside making changes. It would be good if he could have someone alongside him who shared his vision and understood the tasks he had ahead.'

Silence. Arissa couldn't even gulp. What exactly did the Queen mean? Her gaze felt so examining. She patted Arissa's hand. 'You know, he's never brought anyone home for this ball before.'

She turned towards her maid. 'Have you picked something for Arissa yet?'

The maid shook her head. 'Not yet, Your Majesty. That was our next step.'

The Queen pulled her hands back and gave them a little clap. 'Good, I haven't missed the fun part.' She walked up and down the rows, giving the dresses a critical and appraising look. 'No, no, no, too dark, too severe. Too out of fashion.'

The Queen picked out a few dresses. 'This one, this one and, perhaps, this one. Oh, and this one too.'

Arissa was a little stunned and she couldn't help but smile. Every one of the dresses was by a female designer. The Queen waved away the maid and carried the dresses over herself to the curtained area. Red, blue, green and silver. Each one completely different from the other.

She gave a gentle wave of her hand but had an excited gleam in her eyes as she turned around. 'Come on, Arissa, what are you waiting for? Let's try on some dresses.'

Philippe was nervous. He could hear the murmur of voices downstairs. Guests had been arriving for the ball for the last half-hour. His brother and sister were already greeting people on arrival, and normally he would be doing that too. Instead, he'd spent the last thirty minutes immersed in a conference call to three other countries about their maternity services. He was gathering as much information as he could. He had to, if he wanted to make things a success.

He glanced at his watch as he hurried down the corridor towards Arissa's rooms. Her door was wide open and she was silhouetted as she stood at the large window, looking out over the gardens.

His breath caught somewhere in his throat as she spun around towards him. She was wearing a dark green gown with a sequined bodice, gauze shoulders and a fluttering straight tulle skirt. It complemented her skin perfectly. Her only jewellery was a gold choker at her throat. She lifted her fingers to it self-consciously as she took a few steps towards him. 'What do you think? Your mother gave me it to wear.' She glanced downwards. 'Isabella Hugo designed it when she was still up and coming. Isn't it beautiful?' She gave her head a shake, as if she couldn't believe things. 'Your mother was amazing. In fact, she helped me pick this whole outfit.'

She lifted her gaze to meet his. Her hair wasn't coiffed or styled, it was in the natural curls that she always wore and suited her best. She was wearing a little make-up; he could see the mascara opening out her eyes, and the lipstick on her lips. But even wearing the designer dress and the royal jewellery she still looked entirely like Arissa. She still looked entirely his.

'You look amazing,' he whispered as his lips brushed the side of her cheek.

She patted her stomach. 'Thank you, but I'm a bit nervous.'

He took a step back and offered out his arm to her. Right now, what he really wanted to do was kick the door closed behind them both, and keep Arissa all to himself. But this was all part and parcel of what he needed to do next.

He needed to introduce her to the other side of his life. The one that the world would normally see. Tonight was almost like a trial run. She still hadn't told him why she wanted to stay out of the spotlight so much. He didn't want to pry into her life. He wanted her to tell him when, and if, she was ready.

But tonight she would meet his mother's friends and dignitaries from other countries. This ball was always less formal than any other thanks to the privacy surrounding it. He wanted Arissa to be comfortable in his home, and around his family, and this was the best place to start.

His brother and sister were already curious and had only been held off by his excuses of how much work he and Arissa were doing right now.

He smiled. He might have known his mother would manage to circumvent him in one way or another. And the fact that Arissa was currently wearing his great-grandmother's jewellery gave him a feel for how much the Queen must have liked Arissa.

'How did you find my mother?' he asked.

She smiled as she slid her arm through his. 'For a queen, she's surprisingly like most mothers,' she joked. 'But you might have warned me how I was supposed to act around her.'

'Like yourself,' he said quickly. 'And you didn't need any warning. I knew she was going to love you anyway.'

He stopped at the top of the stairs. 'I can see

how much she likes you. That choker was my great-grandmother's. It's one of her favourites.'

Arissa's hands went quickly to her throat as her eyes widened. 'It is? Oh, wow. I had no idea. She never said.'

'She wouldn't.' He looked down towards the ballroom. The music drifted up towards them and people were already circulating in the space below. The waiting staff wore red jackets and ties, or white blouses trimmed with red and black waistcoats. Silver trays were held aloft and the staff moved seamlessly amongst the guests.

Arissa shot him a sideways glance. 'It all looks choreographed. Like some elaborate dance.'

He could sense her nerves and bent closer, tilting her chin up towards his. 'You have nothing to worry about. Tonight is just about mixing with friends. You'll get to meet some of the ministers from the surrounding countries.' A bright laugh carried through the air and Philippe rolled his eyes. 'And you'll get to meet my Aunt Livia, who I guarantee will be the wickedest woman in the room.'

'What about your brother and sister—and your father—what if they don't like me?'

She'd never really seemed nervous like this around him before. He dipped his head and dropped a kiss on her lips. 'They'll love you. Because I do.'

For a second her pupils widened, as if she'd just taken stock of those words. He'd said them out loud without thinking. Something he'd never, ever done in the past. But before he had time to think about it any further there was a noise behind him.

One of the palace staff gave him a nod. 'I'll announce you,' she said briefly.

'Prince Philippe of Aronaz and Dr Arissa Cotter.'

Neither of them had time to think further as all the faces in the ballroom turned upwards to look at them. Arissa slid her arm into his elbow again and he put his hand over hers as they walked down the stairs.

He nodded at a few people on the way down, crossing the ballroom floor towards the area where the King and Queen and the rest of the royal family were congregated.

The crowd parted around them. His brother had an amused grin on his face. His sister was watching Arissa carefully. He could almost see her sizing Arissa up. His mother smiled approvingly and his father stopped the conversation he was in the middle of, to reach out his hands towards them both.

'So this is the lady I've been hearing so much

about. It's a pleasure to meet you, Dr Cotter,' said the King.

Before either of them had time to think, the King had kissed Arissa on both cheeks. His sister's eyebrows rose in surprise then she stepped forward and held out her hand. 'Grace Aronaz,' she said, leaving the Princess title to the side.

'And I'm the good-looking one,' said his brother jokingly as he held out his hand to Arissa too. 'Anthony.' He gave Philippe a glance. 'I think my brother has been hiding you from us all. Trying to keep you secret.' He dipped down low and kissed Arissa's hand. 'It's a pleasure to meet you, Dr Cotter. We hope we'll have a chance to get to know you a little better.' He stepped forward and pretended to whisper in her ear. 'And I have a dozen stories on Philippe that you'll be able to use as blackmail material on him.'

Arissa's eyes were wide. Maybe she hadn't expected such a warm welcome. But Philippe wouldn't have expected anything else from his family.

'It's Arissa, please,' she said finally. 'And it's a pleasure to meet you all.'

The music picked up tempo behind them. The King's eyes gleamed. 'Oh, it's that time again. Right, I'm off to find old Aunt Livia, try and stop whatever trouble she is causing and sweep her around the dance floor while I tell her off.'

Philippe looked at Arissa's surprised face. 'I warned you about her. Wait and see—at various points, each one of us will take her around the dance floor before she ruins any of our diplomatic relationships.'

He watched as Anthony grabbed two glasses of champagne from a tray and moved over next to a blonde woman in a silver gown. Grace turned her attentions to an older woman and launched into a long story. And his mother gave him the slightest nod of her head, which he knew was approval.

He wasn't embarrassed to admit the relief that flooded through his body. All of his family liked her—just as he'd known they would. He could only imagine the questions he'd get later when he was on his own.

He gestured towards the white and black dance floor. 'How are your dancing feet? Do you trust me not to stand on your toes?'

She gave him a nervous kind of smile. Her shoulders had relaxed just a little. 'I guess I could risk it,' she said.

He led her to the dance floor and took her into his arms. It was perfect. The music. The dancing. The lights around them gradually lowered, leaving the ballroom illuminated by flickering candlelight. It was an illusion of course—they weren't real candles, but no one really cared.

They toasted with champagne and ate some of the canapés that were offered. As the sky grew dark outside and the temperature in the ballroom rose, the doors to the gardens were opened. The cooler night air didn't deter people from walking outside.

After her initial few minutes of nervousness, Arissa relaxed. Maybe it was the thought of meeting his parents and family, or maybe it was the whole intimidation factor of appearing at a ball with a prince.

She wasn't used to the life that he had. He'd met Arissa in her own life where she was a capable and competent doctor. Rarely fazed and always able to deal with unexpected emergencies. He'd admired her tenacity and just how capable she was, keeping so many balls juggling in the air at once. Most of all he'd admired her 'can do' attitude.

Tonight there had been a flicker of uncertainty and something else. She'd gripped his arm tighter than she ever had before. Part of him hated that it was him that had put her in this position. He'd almost forgotten how intimidating this could all be to someone who hadn't been brought up in this life.

But Arissa had handled things like a pro. She'd helped him manoeuvre a conversation with a difficult diplomat onto something much less flammable. She'd charmed a few of his mother's friends. He tried his best to ignore the knowing glances they all shot him, smiling and moving on to the next group.

By the time it was almost midnight, he was conscious of the fact Arissa was leaning on his arm. 'You okay?' he asked.

She was staring out at the gardens that had been lit tonight with some pale pink and pale blue lights. 'We could have done with those the other night,' she said dreamily.

'But how would I have enticed you into the maze if everything was clearly lit?' he teased.

One eyebrow rose. 'You enticed me?'

'I think so.'

She gave a shrug. 'Okay, I'll give you that. Maybe you did.' She kept looking out into the dark. 'It's beautiful out there.' She sighed.

'It's beautiful in here too,' he said huskily. She turned to face him, his hands going to her waist. 'You did great tonight. How do you feel?'

'Tired,' she admitted, then gave him a confused glance. 'What—was this some kind of test? What if I hadn't done great?'

He shook his head. 'No. No test. I'd never do that. But this…' he held out his hand to the ballroom behind them '...this is part of my life. It always has been and it always will be. I want you to be comfortable when you're around me, and my family.'

She stayed still for a few seconds, her dark brown eyes staring straight at him. 'Why?' she asked in a croaky voice.

Part of him wanted to cringe. This wasn't the place to have this conversation. He hadn't even really thought things through. He was acting on instinct. But every instinct was telling him the woman in his arms was his highest priority right now.

'Because I want you to stay,' he said.

She flinched. She actually flinched and stepped back out of his arms.

Every part of him recoiled. He'd mistimed things. She wasn't ready to hear anything like this. Or, worst case, she didn't feel the same way.

Arissa put her hand up to her chest. 'But I have things to do, Philippe. I have responsibilities back in Temur Sapora—you know that. I need to find a new job.'

His heart twisted in his chest. He knew all this. He'd known all this before he'd asked her to stay. He'd known all this before he'd told her how he felt.

He wanted to take the words back. Not because he didn't mean them—but because she wasn't ready.

Arissa took another few steps back, nearly tripping over the fabric of her dress. 'I… I… need…'

She looked panicked. He hated that. And he hated more that he'd done it to her.

He held up one hand. 'You need some time. You need some space. You're right. I'm sorry.' He shook his head. 'I should never have said anything.' He gave the slightest dip of his head. 'I'm sorry.'

Then he turned and headed back into the crowded ballroom, letting his professional Prince face slide back into place. Nodding at the right people, making all the right gestures, while all the time his heart was back out on the patio with Arissa, breaking over and over again.

CHAPTER ELEVEN

SHE STARED AT the teapot on the table in front of her. So far she'd had green tea, lemon and ginger and some kind of camomile. None of them had helped the knots in her stomach.

She was sitting bunched up on one of the chairs in her pyjamas with a blanket tucked around her shoulders. She'd seen the sun come up and the gardens gradually come to life.

Her rational brain was doing its best to kick into gear.

When Philippe had looked at her last night all the little jumbled pieces of her brain had slotted into place.

He'd asked her to stay. To stay with him.

It didn't matter it was impossible. It didn't matter it was crazy. What mattered was the intent. The emotion.

It had taken the feet from under her.

Arissa had always been a planner. That was how she'd got through life—meticulous planning. The fact that she'd just had a job pulled from her grasp because of visa details had completely unseated her. Things like that didn't happen to her.

But then, things like Prince Philippe didn't happen to her either.

After a day of being in his company she'd known that she liked him. His easy manner, his flirting, his work with the patients and interest in the people around him hadn't escaped her notice.

As for the kisses…and the electricity between them? She couldn't pretend it wasn't there.

But Corinez was a whole different story. She'd already told him, but he *was* different here. Not in a bad way, just in a more formal way.

Someone knocked on the door. 'Come in.'

The palace press secretary put her head around the door. 'Dr Cotter,' she said warily.

'Come in,' said Arissa again, waving her hand.

The press secretary took a sideways step into the room. She looked as if this was the last place she wanted to be. She was clutching one of the early morning newspapers in her hands. 'I'm sorry,' she said hesitantly.

'For what?' asked Arissa.

The secretary swallowed nervously and stepped forward. 'I think you should maybe go online.'

Arissa blinked as the newspaper unfolded in her hands. Right in the centre of the front page was a picture of her and Philippe. It had been taken last night. She was wearing the gown that was hanging in the corner of the room and the gold choker that was nestled inside the black velvet box on her table. Philippe had his hand on her cheek and was looking down at her, just as she was looking up at him—as if they were the only two people on this planet.

Her breathing stuttered.

While the picture took her breath away, the headline sent a chill over her skin.

Why Is Prince Philippe Hiding His New Bride?

She stumbled to her feet. 'What?'

The press secretary jumped back. 'I'm sorry. There's never been pictures taken at the private ball before. I don't know who would do such a thing. But—' she glanced at the clock; it wasn't even seven o'clock yet '—we have a meeting scheduled in five minutes. We'll release a statement. We'll get to the bottom of this. I just felt I should alert you in the meantime.'

Panic was sweeping over her. Her picture. *Her* picture on the front page of a newspaper.

How long before they found out who she was? How long before they started probing into her background? How long before the headline above her was *Abandoned Baby*? The press secretary glanced at her watch and gave Arissa a sorry nod. 'I'll get back to you,' she said quietly as she left the room.

Arissa started pacing. She couldn't help it. She pulled up her tablet and dabbed in her own name.

Headline after headline.

The Prince's Bride Dressed in Old Queen's Gown.

Arissa Cotter, Who Is She and How Did She Hook the Most Eligible Bachelor in Europe?

She shuddered. It was happening. Her life being picked apart. How far back would they go?

She flicked on the TV. Immediately she saw her name on the ticker tape running along the bottom of the screen.

A woman dressed in a bright pink suit was talking to the news anchor.

'No one has heard of her,' the woman said, throwing her hands in the air. 'Apparently, she's a doctor. But she can't be a very good one. Why else would she lose the job in London?'

If it were possible, her blood ran cold.

Another woman, dressed in a similar suit, on

the other side of the anchor cut in. 'But maybe she doesn't need to be a doctor any more. After all—' she raised her eyebrows '—she's just hooked a prince.'

Arissa leaned forward and put her head in her hands. No. This couldn't be happening.

Sure enough, they jumped from one subject to another.

'We hardly know a thing about her. Do we have a contact in Temur Sapora who could fill in the gaps?'

'The Queen let her wear one of the dresses from her collection *and* a family heirloom. Should we be reading more into this?'

The other woman's eyes gleamed. 'Could this be our new princess?' She clapped her hands together. 'Oh, we need to find out everything. Who her parents are, where she went to school, what her friends say about her.' She leaned forward conspiratorially. 'What her *patients* say about her.'

Arissa thought she was going to be sick all over the pristine carpet beneath her feet. Every part of her skin prickled. Did the woman even realise what she'd just implied? Not only would they invade Arissa's privacy, but they might also invade her patients' privacy.

She grabbed hold of the side of the bed. She actually felt light-headed.

The news anchor cut the conversation with a wide grin. 'I think we'll leave it there before these two start planning their wedding outfits.' He shot a smile to the camera. 'But why don't *you* tell us what you think of this news? You can send us a message on…'

He recited all the ways to contact the news station as Arissa sagged back down onto the edge of the bed.

Philippe opened the door. No knocking. No waiting. He was dressed in a T-shirt and joggers, his face pale and dark circles under his eyes. There was someone else behind him hovering in the corridor outside.

'Arissa? I'm sorry. I had no idea. No idea that someone would take pictures of us.' He glanced towards the TV screen and frowned as he recognised the TV channel.

She shook her head. But before she got a chance to speak he'd crossed the room and wrapped his arms around her.

She was angry. She was upset. No, she was furious. But his actions completely and utterly disarmed her. She'd expected him to be defensive. To be apologetic.

Her body was tense. Every cell lit up in indignation. But his voice was low. She could feel the tremor in it. He was angry too. He was furious.

He waved to the door. 'Give us a minute.'

The door silently closed.

'I know you didn't want this. My family knew you didn't want to be in the public eye. They respected your wishes. I didn't know anything about it until someone came and found me a few minutes ago. When I find out who did this…which one of our friends betrayed us…' She could actually feel him shaking. 'And if I'm angry, they have no idea what my mother will be like. Hell hath no fury like the Queen of Corinez.'

She pushed herself free of his grasp and sat back on the bed. Her head was swimming.

'I want to get away,' she said blankly. 'I want to get away from this place and all the people in it.'

Philippe flinched as if she'd just thrown a punch. She couldn't help her words. She needed to be blunt.

Her hands twisted in her lap. She couldn't get any heat into them at all. Her whole body was freezing.

'Arissa.' He sat down next to her and she held up her hand to stop him talking.

She shivered. 'I need to tell you something.'

She could see he wanted to say so much, but he gave a wary nod of his head. 'Okay.'

'I never told you why I don't want to be in

the spotlight.' She took a few deep breaths. 'It's not for any scandalous reason, or anything that I've done wrong. It's just a part of me that I want to stay private.'

She could tell he still wanted to talk, but she wouldn't let him. She had to finish.

'The safe haven project. There's more than one reason that I'm interested in it.'

'What do you mean?'

Arissa licked her lips. 'I was one of those babies.' She held her breath as she could see the pieces slot into place in his brain.

'What?'

'I was an abandoned baby. The story I told you about one of the babies back home—that was me. I was the baby left outside the old clinic overnight. I was the baby that nearly died. I was lucky, someone found me the next morning and I was treated in hospital. I was adopted by two great people and lived a life where I felt completely loved.' She shook her head. 'But I have no idea who my mother was. I have no idea if she's still alive. I have no idea if having me put her in danger, then or even now. All I know is that I've never gone looking for her, and she's never come looking for me.'

Philippe had gone so pale he looked almost grey. But she couldn't stop talking. Now she'd started she had to get it all out.

A tear slid down her face. 'I understand safe haven in a way that others might not.' She pressed a hand to her chest. 'Sometimes at night I dream of all the reasons a mother would abandon a baby—and not all of them are about the cost of healthcare. What if they're in an abusive relationship? What if having a baby would put them more at risk? What if they've been raped? What if they have mental health issues? What if they are entirely alone and have no support? There are a million reasons why a mother leaves her baby.'

Her hands were shaking now as she tried to keep a handle on her emotions. 'The safe haven project is so important to me. I go hand in hand with it. But what now, Philippe? What if the press dig deeper, they find out my background? What if I become a focal point for them and safe haven is considered some kind of gimmick, instead of the important service we want it to be? What if, when they focus on me, they intrude into my patients' lives and families with sick children start getting harassed?'

She stopped for a second as Philippe's pale face changed into a frown, then lifted her chin and looked him in the eye. 'I won't do that to my patients, Philippe. I won't expose them to that—having a sick kid is hard enough. Plus, I don't want the safe haven project rubbished.'

She put her hand on her chest and looked at him again.

Another tear slipped down her cheek. All those reasons were good reasons. She knew that. But she still hadn't mentioned what was at the heart of it all. She drew herself up. 'But as well as all that, I want privacy, Philippe. I don't want people examining my background. Asking stories around the place I lived when I was a kid. My parents were my parents. That's their spot in my life. They weren't rich. We struggled at times. Do you think I want to be splashed across the papers as the abandoned baby from the poor family? Then I won't be good enough, *they* won't be good enough. I won't have that. I can't have that.' She pointed at the paper. 'These are today's headlines. I can only imagine what they'll say tomorrow if they start digging.'

It was almost as if the world were working against her. A few seconds later she recognised a face on screen. Amal. A little kid she'd worked with in Washington with leukaemia. He was sitting in his wheelchair, beaming at someone. 'I love Dr Arissa,' he said, waving at what seemed like a camera phone.

The feed switched to the news anchor. 'Well, there's a thumbs up from one of her patients,' he said, beaming inanely towards her.

'No,' she breathed as more tears streaked down her face. It was everything she'd feared. 'How on earth did they do that? How did they get hold of Amal so quickly?'

Philippe looked horrified. He glanced at his watch. 'The press pictures must have leaked hours ago when we were all in bed. The story must have gone global.' His brow creased. 'But I have no idea how they found him.'

She turned on Philippe, her voice rising. 'You promised me that there would be no publicity here.' She shook her head, 'And I, like a fool, believed you.' She was angry with herself again. She met his gaze. 'I believed you because I wanted to believe you. Because I trusted you. Because you had me swept up in some kind of—' she threw her hands out in frustration '—made-up fairy tale.'

She walked over to the dressing room and started pulling out her case. Now she'd started she couldn't stop. 'But this isn't for me. This isn't my life.' She couldn't stop shaking her head as she gestured towards the television screen. 'I won't allow them to do that to me—or my patients.'

'Arissa, please stop. I'm sorry. I'm so sorry. I'm sorry that this has happened to you.' He was at her side, holding onto her arm. He looked just as upset as she was.

She'd already flung her suitcase wide and started to throw things haphazardly inside.

Their picture flashed up on the screen together again and she froze. It was that look. That look that had passed between them. His hand on her cheek and her hand on top of it. It made her heart twist inside her chest. There—for all the world to see—was the look of love that had passed between them. It wrenched at her in ways she didn't even want to admit to.

There was another of them midway down the stairs, her arm tucked into his elbow. The smile on his face as he looked at her. One of them dancing in the middle of the ballroom floor with eyes only for each other.

Philippe let out an exasperated sound. 'There's more?'

She'd only seen the first one that had made the newspaper front page. She hadn't seen the rest. Then another flashed up of them on their first day in Corinez, sitting in the coffee shop together, laughing.

He shook his head. 'I thought someone recognised us that day,' he growled.

She'd felt it. She'd felt it every time she was in his company. But now she was seeing it through someone else's eyes. The way they looked at each other, the way they interacted, the way they laughed together, and, instead of making her happy, it made her want to cry.

She couldn't have this. She couldn't live a life that inspected her every breath, her every thought. She couldn't have a life that destroyed the privacy of her patients. She wasn't cut out for this—no matter how much her heart was tearing in two.

Philippe's hand appeared at her arm. 'Let me do something about this. Let me release a statement. I won't let them treat you like this. I won't let them expose your patients like this. They have no right.'

She shook her head. 'But they think they have every right. Isn't that what free speech is about?'

He gestured towards the TV. 'I'll speak to someone at the station. I'll tell them they had no right to use those photographs or to discuss you—or to contact your patients.'

She kept packing her clothes. 'You can't control the world, Philippe. You can't control what people think, and say.' She looked to the TV where the woman in pink was talking incessantly. 'I do a job that I love. I don't want to be pushed out. But I have to protect my patients.' She stepped right up to him. 'I want privacy to live my life. But I *demand* privacy for my patients.' She shook her head. 'And there's no chance of getting it here.'

She gave a wry laugh as another headline flashed up. 'They even had me down as your bride. How ridiculous is that? We've only known each other a few weeks.'

He moved closer, his eyes serious. 'Not that ridiculous.'

Her skin prickled. 'What?'

Philippe sucked in a breath. This day was just snowballing out of control. First the leak, then Arissa's reaction, followed by her revelation. She was an abandoned baby—just like the one he'd treated. The one he'd lost. Arissa could have been lost if someone hadn't come across her. And the thought of that happening made his heart ache. He lowered his head and shook it.

He watched as she continued to throw things haphazardly into her case. Some clothes were missing the case completely. He hated that he'd caused any of this. He was furious that someone from the press had dared to track down one of her patients. She had every right to be angry, and that made him even sadder.

Because all of a sudden, he knew exactly how much Arissa Cotter meant to him. Love. The word he may have mentioned casually, but now he knew just how much he meant it.

After his experience a few years ago he'd thought he'd built an impenetrable wall around his heart. But it seemed he was wrong. Slowly but surely, this beautiful woman with the world of hurt in her eyes had found a way into his heart.

But look what he'd done to her.

He tried to keep his voice steady. 'Where do you plan on going?'

Something flashed across her face. She was angry with him, but she was hurt too.

She shrugged. 'I have no idea.'

He stepped forward and put one hand on the case. 'Wait. At least until tomorrow. The first safe haven cot is getting installed then. Wait and see it through.'

Right now he would try anything to make her stay. Even for one more day. Anything to give himself a bit of time to try and make a plan. A plan to find a way to make things better for Arissa.

He could see from her face that she knew what he was doing. He was trying to use her professional responsibility to will her into staying. 'I'm sure it will all go to plan,' she said, zipping up her case.

'But we need you to see it through. To help with the final touches. The protocols.' He winced. 'The press releases. The way we get the word out there to those that need it, that there is a safe place to leave your baby—no questions asked.'

There was an edge of desperation to his voice that he couldn't even pretend to hide. The woman that had stolen his heart was standing in front of him hurt and confused, all because he'd asked her to come here and work with him.

This was his fault. His.

He should have known better. People had been curious about him all his life. Of course someone would comment about her—particularly if he showed any interest in her. And the truth was he hadn't tried to hide it because he didn't want to.

His family could see it. All of them had given him knowing looks last night.

He'd been proud to show her off. Proud that his family liked her. Touched that his mother had taken such an interest in her and could obviously see how important she was to him, thus welcoming her into the family.

If he'd thought this through, if he'd planned better, he would have spoken to palace advisors. He would have spoken to Arissa about her reluctance to be in the spotlight. He hadn't understood what it meant to her.

And even though it was too late, now he did.

Arissa bowed her head.

'Don't go, Arissa. Not like this. I care about you.' He stepped closer and said words that a few years ago he'd never thought he'd say again. 'You mean too much to me.'

He could tell from the look in her eyes it wasn't enough. The pictures continued to flash up on the screen behind her.

Pictures that captured for the whole world exactly how much he loved this woman.

But he didn't need the pictures to tell him that. The way his heart was squeezing inside his chest told him all he needed to know.

After the longest time Arissa lifted her head. 'I'll stay until tomorrow. I'll talk over the protocols with the staff at the fire and rescue station as the safe haven cot is being installed and make sure they're clear what to do.' She tilted her chin, her voice gaining an edge of determination. 'But I want absolutely no publicity. I'm happy to help draft a statement for the media around the project but that's it. After that I go.'

He'd pulled at her professional responsibilities. But he hadn't pulled at her heartstrings.

He gave a nod of his head. Right now, he would agree to anything that meant he could hold onto her just a few moments longer.

'I'm sorry about your patient. Our press advisors will contact the TV station and put in an official complaint, along with a warning about talking to any of your other patients.' He meant it. He really did. She had a right to her privacy—as did her patients.

And it was up to him to sort this.

'If we're finished, I'd like to be alone now,' Arissa said, her voice stoic.

He gave a brief nod. 'Of course.'

He hated this. He hated every single part of it. He'd exposed the woman he loved to hurt and he wasn't sure how he could fix this—if he could at all.

CHAPTER TWELVE

THE ROOM WAS CLAUSTROPHOBIC. Even though it was beautiful, even though it had views of the expansive gardens, it still felt as if the walls were closing in around her. Every pore in her body right now wanted to get out of here.

But the work was important. They'd moved quickly in Corinez to accommodate the safe haven cot. It seemed that if an order came from a prince, things moved at lightning speed.

An older man knocked and came into the room. He was dressed impeccably in black and held out a hand. 'Jacques Feraunt, Head of Security. I am so sorry, Dr Cotter. But, rest assured, we've discovered the leak.'

She pressed her lips together and tried to ignore the tears that were forming in her eyes. 'You have?'

He nodded. 'It seems that one of our members of staff had been hounded and offered a considerable amount of money to try and capture a photograph of you and the Prince.' He shook his head. 'Regrettably, even though all our waiting staff sign non-disclosure agreements, this individual felt unduly pressured. They had health issues for a family member at home and decided that the money could get them the help they needed.' His face was serious. 'They took the pictures on their mobile phone. We traced them this morning, and they've obviously been dismissed. We will be taking further legal action against them, and the newspapers involved.'

She felt numb. It was as if little creatures were crawling up her arms. She was angry, but the circumstances made her question things.

'What kind of health problems?' she asked.

Jacques looked a little surprised by her question. 'Excuse me?'

'What kind of health problems does the family member have?'

He cleared his throat. 'I believe the member of staff's younger sibling has a form of leukaemia.'

She stood up. 'And they can't get treatment?'

Jacques shifted on his feet. He was obviously trying to choose his words carefully. 'Healthcare in Corinez is complicated, Dr Cotter. None of it is free. Everything has to be paid for.'

She murmured to herself, 'And that's what

Philippe is trying to change with baby steps.' She looked back out over the gardens, her brain mulling over everything she'd heard.

'Can I have the use of a car?'

Now Jacques was definitely surprised. 'A car?'

She nodded. 'I'd like to meet them. The family. The sick kid. This is my speciality. My life's work. If that kid needs to be seen, and a consultation and treatment plan, then I can do that, I can advise. I can do it for free.'

Jacques looked wary. 'I'm not sure that's wise, Dr Cotter.'

She stepped forward. 'You're in charge of security, are you not?'

He nodded. 'Of course.'

'Then I trust you can arrange this. And I trust you can get me where I need to go safely, and without any publicity.'

He gave a brief nod and she lifted her hand to touch the sleeve of his jacket as she tilted her chin upwards. 'I didn't get where I am in this life by always being wise, Mr Feraunt. I got where I am by being compassionate.'

His mother was waiting when he got back to his room. She was dressed impeccably as always and sitting at his desk. She looked over at his rumpled clothes and raised her brows. 'What are you going to do about this?'

'She wants to leave.' He couldn't stop the words hurtling out of his mouth.

His mother drummed her fingers on the desk; it was clear she was thinking. 'Of course she does,' she said quietly. She licked her lips. 'What about you?'

He moved over and sagged into the oversized chair on the other side of the desk. 'What do you mean—what about me?'

She looked straight at him. 'What's the most important thing to you right now, Philippe? What's your priority?'

It was almost as if the world stopped all around him. Everything. No birds singing. No people moving through the corridors of the palace. The stillness amplified in his ears.

It was almost like a magnifying glass on every aspect of his life.

He'd been born a Prince. He'd embraced it for most of his life. He knew what was expected of him. He knew what his place was. The job ahead would be hard—maybe even impossible. He was starting small with maternity services, but eventually he wanted to change his whole country's healthcare system.

Every hair on his body prickled upwards. But he didn't want to do it alone.

The realisation was startling. It shouldn't be. It had gradually crept over him for the last few weeks, ever since he'd met a dedicated doctor with eyes so deep they pulled him in.

He lifted his head to meet his mother's gaze. He wasn't even afraid to say the words out loud.

'My priority is Arissa.'

His mother nodded. 'How would you feel if she wasn't here?'

The words felt like a sword spearing his heart. It clarified so much for him in an instant. 'Like part of me was missing,' he said softly. He met his mother's gaze. 'I don't want to do any of this without her.'

His mother stayed silent for a few seconds, then she stood slowly. 'I suspected you might say that.'

She walked over and put her hand on his shoulder. 'You're old enough to make your own choices, Philippe, and, whatever you choose to do, I will always be your mother, and I will always love you.' She bent close to his ear. 'I don't ever want my children to feel as if part of them is missing,' she whispered in an emotion-racked voice.

She walked back out of his door, closing it softly behind her.

He sagged his head down onto his hands. What had he done? What was he about to do?

Part of his brain was screaming out in protest—reminding him how much he loved his country and being part of it. But the other part was forming plans about what it really meant to love someone completely—and to put them above anything else.

CHAPTER THIRTEEN

THE KID WAS SICK. But in a way it was lucky. She was still at a point where treatment could be very effective—if they were lucky, treatment might even provide a cure.

The family had been more than a little surprised when she'd turned up on their doorstep along with some palace security. After some embarrassment and apologies, Arissa had explained who she was. She wasn't just the Prince's latest girlfriend. She was a doctor—a specialist on kids' blood disorders—and if they'd let her, she'd see their child free of charge and assess what was needed.

With Jacques' help and a quick call to the hospital she'd managed to set up privileges and been able to take the family to a quiet consultation room where she'd had access to equipment and tests. A few hours later, once the X-rays and blood work had been back, she'd been able to sit them down and explain exactly the treatment that their daughter required.

Both of their faces had been pale. She didn't blame them. She'd spent much of her doctor life having these kinds of difficult conversations. But, with the right treatment, this child's chance could be good.

She was still angry about everything that had happened. But she wasn't going to show that to them. She'd taken the time to listen to the circumstances and made the decision that she'd do what she could to help.

It was so easy to judge. So easy to be angry. Occasionally, it was right to be angry. But right now, all she could focus on was the face of the little sick kid in front of her.

It had got her thinking all over again.

By the time she got back to the palace she felt like a giant bag of sand that someone had snipped a little hole in, and the life was just draining out of her.

Her phone buzzed in her pocket and she pulled it out. It took a few seconds for her to scan the email she'd just received. It seemed that even though the research hadn't been published yet, news of their findings had got out. She was the contact name for the clinic so the email had come to her. There had been a huge product licence offer made for their ointment. She blinked, her fingers typing furiously. There was only one thing in her mind. None of the doctors involved in this were in it for the money. This kind of money could secure permanent staff for the clinic in Temur Sapora. She forwarded it on to all involved, along with her suggestion, and held her breath.

But she didn't need to. The replies came in fast and furious. Yes after yes.

At last, something was going right.

She collapsed onto her bed. One more day. That was all she had to last. One more day to finish her duties. Then, she'd need to try and find another position. Maybe she could cover sick leave or maternity leave somewhere? This time she would sort out any visa issues herself.

She rested back on the pillows, trying to focus on her next moves. But, try as she might, her head wouldn't let her concentrate. As fatigue crept over her, her mind circled with the pictures of her and Philippe and the way they had captured how they'd been looking at each other.

It preyed on her senses, making her skin tremble and her stomach churn.

Somehow, the thought of being in Philippe's company tomorrow was making her nervous.

But the thought of leaving this place for good

and never seeing him again? That made her head swim even more and her heart ache in a way she'd never thought possible.

CHAPTER FOURTEEN

THE DAY STARTED AWKWARDLY.

Arissa was ready, dressed in dark trousers and suit jacket, her suitcase sitting in the corner of the room.

Philippe looked as if he hadn't slept. He was dressed impeccably as usual, but his handsome face was marred with dark circles and tiny lines around his eyes.

He seemed nervous. 'Arissa.' The smile he gave her was strained. 'Are you ready? I've talked with the captain at the fire and rescue station and the workmen have just arrived.'

She gave a nod of her head. Jacques was standing behind Philippe and gave her a reassuring smile. She'd asked to keep her actions yesterday private and somehow she knew he hadn't betrayed her.

'Let's go, then.' The words came out a little funny. Almost as if she were really saying, *Be-*

cause I can't wait to get out of here. She still wasn't sure how she felt about everything.

Philippe shot her a pained glance and answered in his polite tones. 'After you.'

She stared out of the window of the blacked-out limousine as they travelled through the city. A casino she hadn't visited. A large white memorial that she'd no idea what it was for. The bustling port filled with cruise ships, and the bus terminal with buses heading up to the ski resort. So many parts of Corinez she hadn't got to see.

Her throat was dry. She couldn't stomach tea this morning. Her hands jittered in her lap, no matter how much she tried to still them.

Philippe cleared his throat. 'The press secretary got a response about the invasion of privacy into your patient.'

She turned to face him.

He spoke slowly. 'It seems that as soon as the story broke on US news and the photos were released, everyone started talking. News stations asked anyone that knew you to phone in.'

Arissa cringed.

Philippe looked carefully at her. 'Amal called the TV station himself. He was excited. He saw his doctor on the TV and wanted to tell them how brilliant she was. He took his mother's phone and just dialled the number on the screen. His mother didn't even know that he'd done it until later.' Philippe gave a gentle shake of his head. 'The TV station asked him to send a clip and he filmed himself. That's why the clip was wobbly.'

Arissa's mouth was open. She couldn't help it. Of course. Kids were so savvy these days on all social media, and Amal was the original cheeky kid. It was exactly the kind of thing he would do. She sagged back in the seat and swallowed. The press hadn't invaded the privacy of one of her patients. It might still not be entirely above board, but Amal had contacted them.

Philippe continued. 'His mother, of course, contacted the station later. But she didn't withdraw permission for them to use the clip.' He paused for a bit. 'We do think there were a few other dubious enquiries regarding some of your patients. We made a complaint to the national press agency and that's been acknowledged and will be followed up.'

Arissa took a deep breath as the car slid to a halt.

She tried to collect her thoughts. Had she overreacted yesterday? Now she knew Amal had made contact himself. But it sounded as if there could still be a few underlying issues. She knew at heart she wouldn't be able to let those go. Ensuring the privacy of her patients would always be at the forefront in her mind. Philippe climbed out of the car and turned, holding his hand out towards her.

She hesitated for the briefest of seconds before accepting his hand and getting out.

The fire and rescue station was busy. The crew were all enthusiastic about the latest project and anxious to help in any way they could.

'Welcome to bedlam!' said the captain, holding up his hands. 'I keep telling them to leave the workmen to get on with it, but they can't stop talking about the project!'

Arissa smiled. Enthusiasm was good. Enthusiasm was something she could harness.

Philippe had moved over and was locked in a conversation with one of the workmen who was standing with a huge sledgehammer, ready to burst a hole in the wall.

'It's great to see Prince Philippe back.' The captain smiled. 'And great that he's finally getting the opportunity to fulfil his role.'

It was the way he said the words and the familiarity of his gaze towards Philippe.

Arrisa couldn't help but ask. 'You know him?'

The captain nodded. 'Since he was a boy. The King and I served together a thousand years ago in the army. We've remained friends. I've watched these children grow up.' He sounded vaguely proud.

Curious, she asked, 'And what do you think?'

He smiled at her. 'About Philippe? He's made for this. He's going to make such a difference. Our health service has needed an overhaul for such a long time. He's so invested in this. After his recent experience no wonder.' He put his hand on his chest. 'At heart, Philippe's a doctor. He'll always think like a doctor and act like a doctor. But for his country?' He nodded slowly. 'He knows what has to be done. He knows how hard it will be. I think free maternity care could make the world of difference in Corinez, and I can't think of a single person who could do the job better than he can.'

Pride. It was there in every word. She could see the admiration in the guy's eyes. The respect.

Part of her ached. Because that was exactly how she felt too. She loved him. She admired him. She respected him. None of what had happened had been his fault. Maybe he should have second-guessed the possibility, but could she really have expected him to, when it hadn't happened before?

Something the captain had said intrigued her. 'What happened before?'

The captain gave her a curious look. 'The

abandoned baby. It was his last patient.' He shook his head. 'Hypothermia. He'd been left in the cold for too long. Philippe was heartbroken. He spent two days in the hospital at the little boy's bedside.'

Her heart twisted. She didn't want to ask. 'What happened?'

The captain shook his head. 'He didn't make it. We found him just too late.' The man sighed. 'That's why this is so important. We can't ever let that happen again. That's why everyone here is so behind this project.'

Now she understood. Now she understood the occasional far-off look in his eyes. Some of the things he'd said—and why he'd been so interested in the safe haven scheme right from the start. It all just made sense.

Her stomach flipped. And her story. Her story must have affected him too. At the moment she'd told him she'd only been thinking about herself, not realising that Philippe understood in a completely different way—he'd lost a baby just like her. Her heart melted. This project linked them both. As she gazed across the room and watched his passion as he spoke to someone it seemed like fate that their paths had crossed. As if it had been written in the stars.

The captain touched her arm and smiled. 'Dr Cotter, are you ready?'

She didn't have time to think any more. Of course. She was here to talk to them about protocols. She could do that. The captain led her towards the staff room; the smell of coffee and cookies was already drifting towards her. Her stomach growled in appreciation. The captain laughed and shouted over to his staff. 'Come on, guys. Our girl is hungry. Let's not keep her from the food.'

She forced herself to smile as the men filed into the room. Philippe was not among them. It was almost as if he was deliberately trying to stay out of her way. The question was—did she really blame him after how she'd acted yesterday? And how could she make it up to him?

It was officially the worst day of his life. Last night he'd written the statement he was currently holding and spent all the hours in between looking over every word.

What he wanted to do was speak to Arissa. But he didn't want to warn her in advance. At some point today there was a good chance she would walk out of his life for ever.

He was determined that wouldn't happen. But he was equally determined that he had to let her follow her own heart. Her happiness meant more to him than anything.

Things at the fire and rescue centre moved

quickly. The workmen literally just smashed a hole in the wall, inserted the premade safe haven cot, then let the technicians ensure it worked exactly the way it should.

As soon as a button was pressed on the outside wall, the cot slid open. A baby could be left inside the cot, along with other items, and the cot closed securely from the outside.

Sensors were everywhere. The cot had lights and heat. It was also accessible from inside the station, so if a baby was placed while the staff were inside, a silent alarm would alert those working. The whole system was designed to give the mother privacy. Nothing alerted until the baby had been left inside and the cot door closed again. From that point on, the fire station silent alarms sounded, along with any attached pagers in case staff were at a fire and rescue situation.

Arissa had made everything go smoothly. She'd reassured all the crew about dealing with a new baby. She'd gone over emergency procedures. Some of the crew had already delivered the odd baby, and knew about the essentials afterwards, but revision was good for everyone.

Links had been established with the local paediatric and social work department to ensure any baby could be quickly checked over then assigned to a temporary foster carer.

Arissa talked with confidence and an easy reassurance—every now and then shooting an anxious glance in his direction. The fire and rescue crew were already enthusiastic; there had only been a few worries, which had easily been ironed out. She told about her own experience of setting up the safe haven cots back in Temur Sapora. She also expressed a sadness that they hadn't managed to find and help all the mothers, but acknowledged that they could only keep an open-door policy in order to protect the privacy and wishes of the mothers.

He listened to every word that she said. Watching her commitment and honesty made him realise the decision he'd made last night was the right one. Things had to be this way.

As the workmen made the finishing touches some invited members of the press started to arrive. Arissa had finished speaking and did her best to fade into the background. That little act still made his insides twist. Every now and then he caught her looking at him. He couldn't work out if she was annoyed with him, or was preparing for her time in Corinez to be over. What he really wanted to do was to go over and put his arms around her. But that wouldn't exactly help her stay incognito. And what Arissa wanted was his first priority.

The captain waved him over as the press settled into their seats. He bent forward and spoke quietly in Philippe's ear. 'I like her,' he said.

Philippe straightened up. The words were unexpected.

'What?'

The captain nodded in Arissa's direction. 'In fact, I more than like her. She's fantastic.' He looked Philippe up and down—in a way that only someone who'd known him all his life could. 'And what's more, I think she's the best thing that could happen to you.'

Philippe's stomach gave a flip. Did he know what Philippe was about to do?

He took a deep breath and looked the captain straight in the eye, a man that knew him better than most. There was a swell of pride in his chest that had been crowded out these last few hours with the fear of letting others down. He took his responsibilities seriously. He looked at the captain's twinkling grey eyes. 'Thank you,' he said proudly. 'I think that too.' He glanced across the busy room towards Arissa. She had her hands folded across her chest as one of the other crew members was talking to her. He had no idea how she'd react to what he was about to do.

But every part of it felt right. He was nervous—and that was unusual for Philippe—but nerves and uncertainty went hand in hand with something new.

Something good.

There was a wave from the front of the room and someone clapped their hands to bring the noise down to a rumble.

Philippe took a deep breath and made his way to the front of the room. His speech was in his pocket—but he didn't need to bring it out. He'd spent most of last night saying it over and over in his head.

He waited until the press members finally stopped talking. He was aware of the inquisitive glances being shot at him. If he gave the press members gathered here today more than half a chance they would bombard him with questions about Arissa.

This was his opportunity to make sure he said what he needed to.

He started quickly. 'Members of the press, I want to thank you for attending today.' He cleared his throat and kept his voice steady. 'You know why I've invited you here today. Over the last few years in Corinez we've had several occasions where an infant—usually a newborn—has been left alone in a public place. Sadly, you all know what happened to the last baby who was left alone, and it's our absolute pledge today to ensure the same thing doesn't happen again. But we also recognise that we have never had services organised to allow a mother to surrender her baby in a safe and anonymous environment.'

He looked up again at the faces fixed on his. 'You all know that I'm a doctor. My greatest wish is that no mother feels as if they have no option but to give up their baby. But I respect an individual's right to choose. Things have changed in the last few years in Corinez, times are hard, and a good friend of mine—' he didn't mention Arissa's name '—enlightened me to the safe haven cot scheme in their country. This scheme is adopted by many countries around the world. France, the USA, Italy, Hungary, Russia, Japan, Switzerland, the Philippines and Temur Sapora in Malaysia, to name but a few. They all run on the same principles that a woman can surrender her baby, no questions asked, with no fear of prosecution.'

He took a few moments as he scanned the faces in the room. 'I wish that we didn't have to do this. But—' he took another breath '—the fact of the matter is, we do.' He held out his hand. 'And we decided that here, at the fire and rescue centre, was the best place to do this.'

He gave a nod as he could see questions forming on the lips of the listeners. 'Our cot has been installed in such a way that a woman can leave her baby someplace warm and safe, and leave without any interference.'

He waited a second. 'We want you to help us get the word out about the new safe haven cot in Corinez. We want everyone to know they can leave their baby in a safe place if they need to do so.'

People started murmuring to each other. One of them shouted out, 'What part did Dr Cotter play in this?'

He could deflect the question. But that wasn't what he wanted to do. 'Dr Cotter has given us the benefit of her own experience of installing a safe haven cot, and has briefed our staff on their roles.'

Other questions started being shouted from all directions but Philippe raised his hand. 'Actually, I'm not finished. I have a further statement you might be interested in.'

His glance went automatically to Arissa, who was watching him from the station kitchen door.

He cleared his throat. 'You all know the challenge that lies ahead. Corinez's healthcare is not currently fit for purpose—it doesn't serve the needs of our population. This safe haven work today is merely the tip of the iceberg.'

He paused to let the listeners consider this. 'My love for my country has always been strong. You all know my intention has been to return to Corinez and take up post as part of our health committee. I have spent the last few years preparing for this role. But recent events have caused me to rethink.'

He kept his gaze steady, fixing on a few in the room who started to shift in their seats uncomfortably.

'Press intrusion is something that my family, and many other royal families across Europe, experience on a daily basis. I have always prided myself on the good relationship that I thought our family had with the press. But the last few days have made me re-evaluate what that means.

'This week I took pride in bringing the woman that I love—a dedicated and competent doctor—to our country and showing her its beauty and introducing her to the people. Dr Cotter is a private person, she wasn't brought up in the media's glare and has no interest in being there. I assured her when she came here, her privacy would be protected.'

He took a long slow breath. 'It seems I was wrong.' Even though he was emotional he kept his voice as steady as possible. Arissa had moved. She had taken a few steps from the edge of the door towards him. He'd just told the world out loud that he loved her, and her eyes were huge.

'I love my country, I always have and I always will, but I'm a person like everyone else in this room—I'm not just a prince, and I believe that one of the greatest gifts you can find as a human being is love. And after thirty-one years, I've found it.'

This time he turned to face her. He couldn't say any of these words without looking her in the eye, because they were all for her.

'I've found a woman who makes my heart sing. I've found someone that got to know me as Philippe—not as a prince. I've found the face I want to see every morning when I wake up, and every night before I close my eyes. I've found the person I want to spend the rest of my life with, and I'm willing to make sacrifices in order to be with her.'

Arissa's mouth opened. She took a few steps forward.

'The tasks I have ahead are huge—a lifetime's work. My plan was to start—with the agreement of the health committee—on introducing free maternity services within Corinez. And what's abundantly clear is that if I'm to do those tasks, I need the love and support of someone by my side who understands exactly the breadth of my role. I want to work in partnership with the person I love, because I want this to last a lifetime.'

He swallowed, his throat becoming tight, and turned back to face the press. 'Yesterday, we learned that some of Arissa's previous patients had been approached by the media. These issues have been raised with the Independent Press Standards Organisation. Patient-doctor privilege and confidentiality is sacred. No doctor would ever want to expose their patients to invasion of their privacy. Arissa came here because of me. The press is interested in her because of me. She now feels, because of this intrusion, she won't be able to function as a doctor. And if she wants to leave, then I'll be leaving with her.'

He heard her small cry to his side as the press erupted in front of him.

'You can't do this!' one of the reporters shouted.

'What will the King say? The Queen will be furious!' shouted another.

'Who approached the patients?' said another, looking angrily around. 'We'd never do something like that.'

Philippe didn't hesitate. He looked from one to the other. 'I can, and I will. I have spoken to the Queen and have her complete approval. Like any mother on this planet, her overwhelming wish is that her child is happy. The rest of the royal family have given me their unwavering support. Do we really want to examine what the effects of the press attention have resulted in for other royal families? Arissa isn't here to be a princess. She's here to be a doctor. I suggest that we let her.'

He nodded to the reporter who'd shouted out last. 'And I thank you for respecting patient confidentiality.'

The reporter glanced at his neighbours. 'Any self-respecting reporter would do the same. Let's face it,' he said, 'we'll all be a patient ourselves at some point.'

Philippe's voice had gathered strength. He was determined. He could see a few panicked expressions.

'Philippe.' The voice was almost a whisper.

She was at his side, her eyes wet with tears. Her arms folded across her body. 'You can't give up being a prince for me,' she said with a shaking voice.

He smiled and stepped down, sliding his hand into her hair. 'I can. And I will. Tell me where you want to go and I'll come with you. I'll work anywhere in the world. If you want to go back to Temur Sapora permanently, then I'll come with you.'

He could hear the noise roaring behind him.

The multiple conversations. Reporters phoning their editors and TV stations.

He ignored every single part of it. The only thing that was important was the woman standing straight in front of him. The woman with the big brown eyes and trembling lips. He didn't have a single doubt about that—and that told him everything he needed to know.

It felt as if she were watching a movie of someone else's life.

Every word peeled back another of the layers she'd shielded herself with.

The role he'd been destined for. Trained for. Prepared for. He was ready to give it all up for her. For love. And he'd told the world.

She'd wanted to talk to him. She'd wanted to talk to him about some of his suggestions for change, and about the possibility of her helping to create a service for kids like the one she'd seen yesterday. The need was there. It could be the next step in the plan. She could make a difference. Wasn't that what a doctor was for? As long as her patients were protected. Some of the responses in the room were actually heartening. She could see others agreeing with the reporter who'd spoken out last. Maybe raising this issue out loud today, and the report to the IPSO, would be enough to make this stop.

'I wish you'd told me about the baby that died, Philippe. I know how much that must have affected you.'

He blinked and nodded. 'It almost broke me. It's the reason I ended up in Temur Sapora. I was feeling lost when I got there. I knew the job I had to come back and do, and then…' he smiled '…I met you. And it felt like fate. From the very start. Your story and mine, Arissa.' He bent forward and whispered in her ear. 'I know that for others this might seem rash. But nothing about us feels wrong. And I'll do everything I can to make us work.' The fingers in one of his hands intertwined with hers.

She stopped thinking about the other people in the room and put her hand up and touched Philippe's face. 'You have so much work to do here, Philippe. Who else can do it with the passion and dedication that you can? No one else knows this place like you do.'

'I won't have you feeling the way you did the other day. Not because of me. I love you, Arissa. I spoke to my mother last night. She completely understands. She wants me to follow my heart, and my heart is you.'

A tear slid down her cheek. She'd never felt so loved by a man. So wanted. Her hand slid over his. 'But can you be happy if you aren't here?'

'What I need in this life to be happy is you, Arissa.'

His gaze was so sincere. He wasn't sad. He was smiling. It was almost as if saying the words out loud and making his declaration had taken a weight off his shoulders.

A shout came from the side.

'Corinez needs this reform. The healthcare system has to change. The people of Corinez can't trust anyone as much as they trust you.'

'The Independent Press Standards Organisation will get to the bottom of this. It won't happen again.'

'Arissa, what can we do to persuade *you* to stay?'

The question came from an older man with grey hair. Arissa's skin prickled. The attention was on her.

For a few seconds she couldn't think straight. Then her focus shifted to the man she loved standing in front of her. He'd offered to give up everything for her. What could she give up for him?

Or maybe she didn't need to give up anything, maybe she needed to compromise. That didn't seem quite so terrifying.

She stared at the podium with the microphone. Maybe it was time to take control. To tell her own story. To use the press attention to bring the focus entirely on the safe haven scheme and its value. If she owned her story and told it herself then she wouldn't need to worry about the press revealing it to the world for her.

She closed her eyes for a second and concentrated on the heat of Philippe's skin next to hers. The strength. The passion. This was hers. This was hers to take.

She straightened her back and relaxed her shoulders, purposely pushing them down.

She squeezed Philippe's hand and kept holding it as she stepped up to the podium. She could do this. She could do this for her, and for him.

What kind of life did she want? One where she had to live a life without the man that she loved? Or one where she faced the world and told them the truth?

There it was. She'd admitted it to herself—even though she'd known it for the last few days.

He had more strength and determination than she could ever have dreamed of. He could have walked away from someone like her. Walking away from his country might have never even entered his head. But for Philippe, it had. He was clear. He would stand up for her no matter what.

He tugged at her arm. 'Don't. You don't need to say anything. Don't be forced into the spotlight—I know that's not what you want.'

She reached back and touched his cheek with her free hand. 'Maybe we can both get what we want,' she whispered.

She stood behind the podium and faced the press. They silenced much quicker for her than they had for Philippe.

She lifted her chin. 'Prince Philippe is right. I'm a doctor. That's what I am and what I want to continue to be. But I have a story to tell you. One that I preferred to keep private. But somehow—' she glanced around the room at the expectant faces '—it seems that today might be a good day to tell it.'

She took a few moments to collect her thoughts. 'I was an abandoned baby. Thirty years ago I was left outside an unmanned clinic in Temur Sapora.' She tilted her chin upwards. "'I was lucky. I was found. I was sick, but recovered in hospital and was adopted by a loving couple who gave me the best life they could.' She gave a little smile. 'I miss and think about them every day.'

She could see the exchange of glances.

'And here I am. I've grown up, trained as a doctor and now I specialise in children's blood disorders, with a particular focus on cancers. I know there's a need in Corinez. I saw a patient only yesterday who needs accessible treatment that could save their life.' She put her hand on her chest. 'What will it take for me to stay? I know you only ask because you want to keep your Prince. I don't want to keep a prince.' She turned and met his gaze. 'I want to keep the man I fell in love with, Philippe Aronaz.

'I want you all to publicise the safe haven cot. I want you to tell how it can save lives. I want you to reassure women that there is someplace safe that they can leave their babies. And...' she paused and smiled at Philippe '...if the plans for maternity care work out, maybe we will be able to offer all kinds of support to women in need.' She took a final breath. 'And it goes without saying that I expect integrity from every person in the room to respect the rights of any patients that I see.'

His hand moved, releasing her fingers as he changed position and came and stood at her back, slipping one hand over hers. It was almost as if he was moving into a protective stance—and somehow that gave her the reassurance that she needed.

He was there. He was with her. Confidence flowed throughout her body. She turned to face Philippe instead of the press. 'Do you think this can work?'

He leaned forward and put his forehead on hers. It was as if they were the only two people in the room. They weren't surrounded by TV cameras. There wasn't an array of hungry press people in the room. 'Are you sure, Arissa? I love you. I'll go anywhere with you. I mean that. Don't do anything that will make you unhappy. I don't want that for you.'

He blinked and his long eyelashes brushed against her skin and sent tingles to every part of her. 'Will you be my champion?' she whispered back.

A smile broke out across his face. 'Always,' he murmured.

'Then, we do this together. We can make this work.'

For a few seconds neither of them moved, but then Philippe raised his head, slipped his hand into hers and turned to face the press pack.

'Our press conference for today is over. I think you have what you need. Today is a unique opportunity for us all. Please spread the word about the safe haven scheme and our plans for maternity care.'

It was a moment in history. It had never been her intention to be in this situation but at this second she couldn't be prouder of the man that she loved.

Yes, life would change. But it would change

hand in hand with a man that she wanted to be by her side for the rest of her life.

Philippe turned towards her. 'We need to do something,' he said quickly, grabbing her hand and pulling her towards the staff room in the fire and rescue centre.

She was stunned. He ushered the few people that were in the room back outside and closed the door quickly behind them.

'What's wrong?' What on earth was he doing?

He shook his head and stepped up close. 'Nothing is wrong.' He laughed as he glanced around them, then reached up and touched her cheek. 'I always thought when I did this I would plan. There would be stars. There would be a romantic dinner. A beautiful setting. Maybe even some music.' He held his hands out. 'Instead we have a slightly messy staff room, with a few odd chairs.'

Her stomach flipped. Somehow she knew what was going to happen next. Her heart swelled in her chest as she tried to catch her breath.

Philippe dug down into his pocket and opened a black velvet box as he dropped to one knee. 'Arissa Cotter, I love you. More than I ever knew was possible. You've taught me to trust and love again. I promise that no matter where this road leads I'll be by your side. If we choose to stay here, then know that I also want to help you with your work in Temur Sapora. When you go there, I'll go there. I want to mirror your commitments to your own country. It's part of you, therefore it's part of me. I want you to—'

She bent forward and put a finger to his lips. 'Stop talking, Philippe.' A millisecond of worry flashed across his eyes before she laughed and shook her head. 'My answer is yes. I love you. I love what you just did for me. I love what you've promised me. I hope we never have to leave, but if we do, I'll be leaving with the man I love.' She ran her fingers through his hair. 'I don't care where we are, just as long as we're together.' She glanced down at the ring and her eyes widened. 'Where on earth did you...?'

He pulled the ring from the box. 'This was given to me last night by my mother. It's a family ring, belonged to a former queen.' He slid the yellow-gold ring with a huge square green emerald onto her finger. 'My mother said that as soon as she saw you in that green dress, she knew this ring was meant for you.'

Arissa sucked in a breath as her eyes filled with tears. 'She gave it to you, even though she knew you might leave?'

He nodded as he pulled her towards him. 'They love you, Arissa. Just as much as I do.'

He walked to the door and opened it for the briefest of seconds. 'She said yes!' he shouted before slamming the door closed and pulling her back into his arms.

And as her husband-to-be kissed her, she forgot all about the cheers outside.

EPILOGUE

'READY?'

Arissa nodded as Philippe's sister, Grace, bent forward to give her a kiss on the cheek. 'See you in a minute, then,' she whispered as she sashayed down the aisle in front of her in her navy maid-of-honour dress.

Arissa breathed in. The music had started. It was time to go.

She stared down at her yellow and orange flowers. A slightly unusual wedding bouquet with half the flowers native to Temur Sapora and half native to Corinez.

She took a deep breath again to relax herself. They were in the private palace chapel. The world knew the wedding was taking place today, but they also knew it was only being attended by family and friends. The press had been promised a kiss from the newly-weds on the palace balcony later.

Her cream lace bodice gown with satin skirts

had been chosen with help from the Queen. As the music continued she stepped out onto the aisle.

Sun was streaming through the stained-glass windows at the end of the chapel. But she couldn't focus on the sun. All she could focus on was her handsome prince standing at the end of the aisle, filling out every inch of his dress uniform.

As she reached him he mouthed the words to her, 'You're stunning,' as he lifted her veil and arranged it behind her tiara, which belonged to his mother.

Everything had worked out perfectly. She'd been working at the local hospital for more than a year now—with little interference from the press. The safe haven cot had seen two babies left there—but that was good, because the message was out there. The research from Temur Sapora had finally been published with her name near the bottom of a large list of doctors. But that wasn't the best part. Philippe had helped her set up a non-profit charitable organisation. The ointment had gone into worldwide production helping people around the globe, with profits now feeding into various charities—as well as the clinic in Temur Sapora.

Most importantly, six weeks out of the year saw them both head back to her island to work in the clinic, swim in the sea and sit on the beach. It was the reality check they both needed. It helped them conquer the overwhelming pressures of trying to build a new health system in Corinez.

The music stilled, and Philippe intertwined his pinky with hers as the minister started the service. 'My champion,' he whispered.

She met his gaze and squeezed gently. 'My champion. For always.' Then she bent forward to kiss her husband-to-be. She didn't want to wait a second longer.

* * * * *